Things We Do Not Talk About

Also by Daniel A. Olivas

The Book of Want: A Novel (2011)

Anywhere But L.A.: Stories (2009)

Latinos in Lotusland: An Anthology of Contemporary Southern California Literature (2008), editor

Benjamin and the Word / Benjamín y la palabra (2005)

Devil Talk: Stories (2004)

Assumption and Other Stories (2003)

The Courtship of María Rivera Peña: A Novella (2000)

Things We Do Not Talk About

Exploring Latino/a Literature through Essays and Interviews

Daniel A. Olivas

San Diego State University Press

2014

Things We Do Not Talk About: Exploring Latino/a Literature through Essays and Interviews by Daniel A. Olivas is published by San Diego State University Press.

Information regarding the images/portraits that appear in this volume appear here:
http://sdsupress.sdsu.edu/danielolivas/olivas_foto_credits.html

San Diego State University Press
5500 Campanile Drive
Arts and Letters 226, mailcode 6020
San Diego, CA 92182-6020

sdsupress.sdsu.edu
facebook.com/sdsu.press
http://bit.ly/sdsu_press

Cover painting, "Coatlique," by Perry Vasquez

Book Design by Guillermo Nericcio García
for memogr@phics designcasa.

ISBN-10: 193853705X
ISBN-13: 978-1-938537-05-9

FIRST EDITION PRINTED IN THE UNITED STATES OF AMERICA

As always, for Sue and Ben

Source Acknowledgments

The following essays appeared previously, sometimes in slightly different form, and are reprinted by permission of the author:

"Great Expectations" (*LatinoLA*, 2004); "Cuento de Fantasma" (*The Elegant Variation*, 2005); "Documenting Hate" (*Jewish Journal*, 2005); "A Pocho in West Hills" (*The Raven Chronicles*, 2005); "Still-Foreign Correspondent" (*Tu Ciudad*, 2006); "Writers Write. Period." (*La Bloga*, 2006); "Moving from Tight Little Machines to the Novel" (*California Authors*, 2007); "Czech Teen's Words and Art Put a Face on the Holocaust for Me" (*The Jewish Journal*, 2007); "Exploring the Mexican American Experience" (*California Lawyer*, 2008); "My Second Act as a Writer" (*Daily Journal*, 2010); "Valley Chicano Writer Explores the Holocaust" (*Jewish Journal*, 2010); "The Priest That Preyed" (*The New York Times*, 2013).

The following interviews appeared previously, sometimes in slightly different form, and are reprinted by permission of the author:

Luis Alberto Urrea (*The Elegant Variation*, 2005); Salvador Plascencia (*The Elegant Variation*, 2006); Aaron A. Abeyta (*La Bloga*, 2007); Daniel Alarcón (*The Elegant Variation*, 2007); Margo Candela (*La Bloga*, 2007); Myriam Gurba (*La Bloga*, 2007); Manuel Muñoz (*La Bloga*, 2007); Sam Quiñones (*La Bloga*, 2007); Helena María Viramontes (*La Bloga*, 2007); Gustavo Arellano (*La Bloga*, 2008); Aaron Michael Morales (*La Bloga*, 2008); Gregg Barrios (*La Bloga*, 2009); Michael Luis Medrano (*La Bloga*, 2009); Carmen Giménez Smith (*La Bloga*, 2009); Susana Chávez-Silverman (*La Bloga*, 2010); Francisco Aragón (*La Bloga*, 2010); Octavio González (*La Bloga*, 2010); Ray González (*La Bloga*, 2010); Rigoberto González (*La Bloga*, 2010); Ilan Stavans (*La Bloga*, 2010); Héctor Tobar (*La Bloga*, 2011); Sergio Troncoso (*La Bloga*, 2011); Richard Blanco (*La Bloga*, 2012); Carlos E. Cortés (*La Bloga*, 2012); Sandra Cisneros (*Los Angeles Review of Books*, 2012); Reyna Grande (*Los Angeles Review of Books*, 2012); Rubén Martínez (*Los Angeles Review of Books*, 2012); Justin Torres (*Los Angeles Review of Books*, 2012).

Acknowledgments

As with each of my books, my efforts would yield nothing without the love, support and thoughtful suggestions from many others.

Mil gracias to San Diego State University Press for seeing the merits of this project. I hope that it will be used by all students and other lovers of Latino/a literature for many years to come.

I thank the editors and publishers of the print and online publications where my essays and author interviews first appeared. Because of you, this book started to come to life—word by word—during the last decade.

To those remarkable Latina and Latino writers I interviewed and whose words appear in this book, I thank you for giving us, your readers, powerful and eloquent literature to enjoy and learn from...may you all continue to write for many years to come.

Always to my parents, Miguel ("Mike") and Isabel ("Liz") Olivas, who gave their five children a love of literature and the opportunity to attend wonderful schools.

To our son, Benjamin Formaker-Olivas, who fills us with joy as he becomes a proud, educated, and caring young man.

Finally, to my beautiful and brilliant wife, Sue Formaker, who these last three decades has made my life what it is: wonderful! I love you with all my heart.

Contents

Introduction

In assembling the essays and author interviews that appear in this collection, I came to the realization that in my life as a fiction writer, poet, and book critic, I have spent a rather large portion of my energies obsessing about the creative process of writing itself. Perhaps it is my lawyer's training that compels me to explore the who what-when-where and why of creating literature.

As you will see when you enter the pages of this book, my focus has not been solely on my own creative process. For many years, I have asked other writers about their artistic and practical approaches to creating stories, poems, essays and plays, and as a Chicano writer, I have been particularly interested in what we generally call "Latino/a literature" and how others help in creating works that make up our canon.

In rereading the dozen essays that make up the first section of this volume, I am struck by my concern with the "moral authority" I may or may not possess to explore certain themes through my fiction and poetry. For example, in the essays "Documenting Hate" and "Valley Chicano Writer Explores the Holocaust," I question my ability (as a Jew-by-choice) to write fiction that honestly and authentically addresses anti-Semitism. As you will see, my family's encounter with a hate crime settled the matter for me.

Other essays touch variously on my attempt to move from short stories to the novel, signing and selling books, and offering tough love to aspiring writers. Then there's the juggling: balancing the writer's life with parenthood and a demanding "day job" as a government attorney. Lurking behind each piece are questions. What does it mean to be a Chicano writer? What do readers expect from me? What do I expect from myself? Finally, my op-ed piece for *The New York Times,* which begins this book, addresses how I attempted to use fiction to confront the sexual-abuse scandal that has been rocking the Roman Catholic community with a particularly painful turn for the Latino community. Taken as a whole, I believe my essays will offer a glimpse into both the creative and practical sides of writing from one author's viewpoint.

This volume's second section saves this book from falling into a solipsistic abyss. There, I collect 28 interviews I have conducted of Latina and Latino writers at various stages of their careers. For example, we have Luis Alberto Urrea explaining that he decided to fictionalize his great-aunt's life in the magnificent novel, *The Hummingbird's Daughter* (2005), because "you can't footnote a dream." There is Helena María Viramontes explaining why her latest novel delves deeply into the hardships of her Chicana protagonists: "I marvel, truly marvel, at the everyday, ordinary ordeals of human life, and I want to give justice to an existence that very few people or readers acknowledge." Poet Carmen Giménez Smith offers this lovely sentence: "I am enthralled by syntax, by the sinews of the sentence," and we witness the indomitable Sandra Cisneros admitting: "I'm not an expert on anything, not even me. That's why I write."

I have been delighted to discover that these interviews—all of which first appeared online in literary websites—have been relied upon by scholars as they analyze and discuss the works of some of our most acclaimed authors. For example, my interview with Daniel Alarcón was quoted and included as a bibliographical source in the well-received *Encyclopedia of Contemporary Writers and Their Work* (2010) by Geoff Hamilton and Brian Jones. Similarly, Ellie D. Hernández cites my interview of Gustavo Arellano in her scholarly dissection of borderland identities in *Postnationalism in Chicana Literature and Culture* (2009). Quite by accident, I also learned that students have used these interviews in their high school, college, and graduate studies. All of this convinced me that the interviews have already played an important role in the scholarly understanding of Latino/a literature.

As you read each interview, keep in mind that the responses are frozen in time. That is to say, the authors very likely would not give precisely the same answers today. Indeed, when reviewing their interviews for the completion of this book, more than one felt a bit embarrassed by the responses—for no reason, as far as I'm concerned. But everyone evolves, and it's not surprising that several of my subjects see their craft a bit differently now. Second, all of the authors have continued to publish and gain further recognition for their art. Indeed, one (Richard Blanco) made rather dramatic history when President Barack Obama chose him to be the first Latino and openly gay man (not to mention the youngest) to serve as the inaugural poet for the President's second term. All have made history in their own right and deserve to be recognized, read, and studied.

What might you, the reader, gain from this book? Well, you will certainly get a glimpse into the manner by which I approach writing, culture, and the vagaries of life. No doubt, you will see how some of our most successful contemporary authors consider such issues in sometimes wildly differing manners. In the end, I simply hope that readers will feel as if they have a deeper understanding and appreciation of this thing we call Latino/a literature.

—Daniel A. Olivas,
West Hills, CA | March 24, 2014

ESSAYS

The Priest That Preyed

The New York Times (2013)

It is the autumn of 2003, and I am sitting with my wife and teenage son at a large table that is groaning with plates of Mexican food and soft drinks and wine. We're celebrating my sister's anniversary, and like most Mexican parties in Los Angeles, a member of a religious order is in attendance to share in the family's joy.

This time, it's a nun whom I've known since I was a student at St. Thomas the Apostle grammar school. I am no longer Catholic, but I admire this tough, compassionate woman who dedicated herself to educating the children of my predominantly working-class Latino neighborhood. She leans over and says, almost in a whisper, "I read your new book." And then she says, "I recognized him."

Immediately, I know whom she's talking about, and I begin to perspire.

The title story of the book, called "Assumption," describes a fictionalized priest, Father González, who served a parish in a neighborhood not unlike the one I grew up in. The priest in the story is known for being "cool" and spending time with some of the more troubled boys at the nearby grammar school. The boys talk about how he has invited them to visit his room, drink wine, listen to Sly Stone and look at dirty magazines. These visits, of course, lead to the boys' molesting. In the story, the priest gets caught and, in disgrace, hangs himself.

In real life, shame did not bring an end to the abuse. The priest I based the story on, the priest the sister recognized, was the Rev. Eleuterio Ramos. My parish knew him as Father Al, the hip young priest who spoke out for immigrant and Chicano rights, railed against the Vietnam War, could drink with the best of them and dedicated his spare time to mentoring the most troubled boys at St. Thomas.

"I was young and naïve," the nun says. "I thought it was great that he was helping the boys who needed it." She looks down at her plate. Finally she says, simply, "I liked your book."

I, too, was naïve. I was jealous of the boys who got to spend extra time with Father Al. He took some of my friends to the beach, the movies or to his famous room at the rectory. But I came from a home that had two attentive parents, not the profile Father Al searched out.

The allegations against Father Al, who became a priest in 1966 and was transferred from parish to parish 15 times, first came out in the '90s, when the Orange Diocese was sued by two men. They accused Father Al of plying them with alcohol when they were children, showing them adult films and sexually abusing them. But by that point, he had already been suspended from priestly duties. In 2003, he admitted to the police that he had molested at least 25 boys. But because of the statute of limitations, he was never charged, and he died in 2004, a year after my conversation with the nun.

According to church records that became public last month after years of litigation brought by victims of sexual abuse at the hands of priests and brothers of religious orders, this story is sadly familiar. The documents include information on 124 priests over four decades, and demonstrate a pattern by the church of cover-up, denial and—I can't help but think it—evil.

Though Father Al's victims were not only Latino, the news has been particularly painful to Latino families who considered Father Al to be one of them. Families like mine admired his desire to help the most vulnerable in the Catholic community, the troubled boys who were poor or lacked a father figure. That admiration blinded us to the clues that, today, would not go unquestioned.

The same is true for Father Al's superior, Cardinal Roger M. Mahony of Los Angeles, who was famous among Latinos for speaking out for immigrants' rights. But as the thousands of pages of records show, he apparently tried to prevent law enforcement from discovering the abuse of his parishioners. But this question of guilt should be decided in a court of law. Last week, the retired cardinal was relieved of his remaining duties.

Thinking back to that conversation with the nun a decade ago, I have no doubt that more revelations will come to light; earlier this week it emerged that the church hadn't released all the information it had promised.

I once hoped that fictionalizing Father Al would help expose the truth to a community that had been so thoroughly betrayed. But I have now come to the conclusion that fiction can never match the audacious brutality visited upon those children for so many years.

Documenting Hate
Jewish Journal (2005)

In late fall of 1999, I wrote a short story, "Summertime," which I eventually included in my collection, *Assumption and Other Stories* (2003).

When the book reviews started coming in, most noted that particular story's unsettling premise. But what fascinated me more was the response I received via e-mail or in person from family, friends and strangers alike. More on that later.

"Summertime" begins benignly enough. The first section of the story has the heading, "6:53 a.m.," and we encounter a married couple having difficulty getting their young son ready for summer day camp. Claudio Ramírez and Lois Cohen obviously love their son, Jon, but as with most parents who must get to work, mornings can be a bit frustrating. Jon eventually gets dressed, fed and trundled off to Claudio's car for the ride to camp. The next section is titled, "7:39 a.m.," and we switch to a dusty, small hotel room where we meet a sleeping man named Clem whose "head looked like a pot roast as it lay nestled heavily on the over-bleached pillowcase." Clem wakes to begin his day. Clem is from Oregon and has driven to Southern California on a mission.

The story moves along, switching between the Ramírez-Cohen family and Clem. We eventually learn that Clem's "mission" is to perpetrate a hate crime. He eventually settles on the Jewish day camp that Jon attends. I paint Clem as an average person who feels belittled by the world and who hopes to have a "big day" that will put his face in every newspaper and on TV. He is no evil genius. But the evil he perpetrates is as harrowing and real as any better-planned hate crime.

I wrote the story after we experienced the horror of Buford Furrow's attack at the North Valley Jewish Community Center (JCC), on August 10, 1999. Furrow, a self-described white separatist, shot and wounded three children, a counselor and the receptionist at the JCC. That same day, he murdered a Philippines-born postal worker, Joseph Santos Ileto. Furrow admitted to wanting to kill Jews. He also stated that Ileto was "a good 'target of opportunity' to kill because he was 'non-white and worked for the federal government,'" according to then-U.S. Attorney Alejandro Mayorkas.

For almost four hours that hot, horrible day, my wife and I didn't know if our 9-year-old son, Benjamin, had been a victim. We huddled together with my mother-in-law outside the camp waiting for word. Unfortunately, because the police were concerned that the shooter or shooters were still in the vicinity, the children who had not been wounded had been whisked off to a safe house. A rumor ran through the crowd that a boy named Benjamin had been shot and killed. The agony ended only when, eventually, we were reunited with our son.

Frankly, I'm having difficulty writing these words because the memories are coming back, full and clear. But that's one reason I wrote "Summertime." I wanted to use fiction to remind others that ordinary people living in today's world can be the target of hate crimes. And I also wanted readers to understand how easily hate-filled doctrines can be appropriated and acted upon by an "average" person.

Now back to the various responses to "Summertime." Most readers—particularly those who know my family—knew that Clem was based on Furrow. But several other readers had never heard of Furrow's attack on the JCC or his murder of Ileto. Those readers (most of whom do not live in California and who are not Jewish) expressed shock when I mentioned that the story was based on our own experience that day in August. And I expressed shock that they had not heard of the incident, particularly since it had received extensive (if not worldwide) news coverage. But this confirmed my conviction that writing about hate—even if fictionalized in a short story—can indeed educate the public about how easy it is for a person to become a Buford Furrow.

When I started writing fiction in 1998, I didn't feel that I had the moral authority to write about anti-Semitism. Though I had converted to Judaism ten years earlier, my experience with bigotry was based on my ethnic identity as a Chicano. But after August 10, 1999, I earned the right to talk about one particular act of hate against Jews. I will go further: I now have the duty to remind others of what Furrow did that day. Why? Because if we forget, we help create a climate where it could happen again and the Furrows of the world will have won. And I don't intend to be responsible for that.

Moving from Tight Little Machines to the Novel
California Authors (2007)

I recently interviewed Salvador Plascencia on the occasion of the paperback release of his novel, *The People of Paper* (2005). I asked if he was working on another novel or perhaps short stories.

He replied: "I think I'm stuck writing novels for better or worse. I'm too scattered to be able to make one of those tight little machines they call short stories."

Tight little machines? Perfect.

But what struck me more than Plascencia's eloquence was his unapologetic candor. At the time, I was in the midst of trying to make the leap from short-story writer to novelist, and going crazy in the process. Plascencia got me wondering why I was putting myself through all that angst. I'd garnered nice reviews for my two collections, *Assumption and Other Stories* (2003), and *Devil Talk* (2005), and my stories have been taught in high school and college. My novella and children's picture book were also well received. I write because it gives me joy, not because it'll put food on the table. I had no compelling reason to start writing a novel.

When I started writing, why did I gravitate to short stories rather than the novel? Part of the answer is the delight I derived when I was younger and falling in love with those tight little machines by such writers as Fitzgerald, Maugham and Hemingway. And then later, I discovered the likes of Boyle, Cisneros and Bender. I learned that a short story is like a poem: each word, every sentence, has to matter. Yet I could think of a few great 500-page novels that might be trimmed by a few thousand words without losing much strength.

Another reason why I gravitated to the short form was my busy schedule as a full-time litigator with the California Department of Justice. I'm also a husband and father. The spotty writing time that I can scrape together in the evenings or weekend mornings makes it difficult for me to maintain any sort of continuity for longer pieces. I know other writers can do it, but we all have different strengths, as my mother always reminded me when I was young. I figured that I could write short stories for the rest of my life and that would just fine, thank you very much. There was no disgrace in being a short story writer. I mean, Borges never wrote a novel, right?

I completed another short-story collection, which my agent and I sent out. But a couple of large publishing houses passed on it with basically the same sentiment: love your writing but short stories are a tough sell. Don't you have a novel in you?

This was a bit maddening because, as all writers know, no one ever asks a novelist, "Don't you have a short-story collection in you?" Never. Ever. But that's fine. There are greater injustices in life.

In any event, since I like challenges, I tried to map out the kind of novel I would write. And this is when I started to go a bit crazy. Visions of writing the "Great American Novel" crept into my brain. Once that happened, the very idea of writing a novel seemed like an impossible—and not very fun—job. And then I conducted the Plascencia interview, which shook some sense into me. I suddenly realized that I would not write a novel unless it was fun. If I decided not to move to the longer form, that was fine. So I figured I'd take baby steps. If I were to write a novel, what would be about?

I've written about Chicanos of all ages and income levels who confront various challenges from unrequited love to battles with bigotry or economic hardship or you-name-it. I've also set stories in Mexico and I haven't been afraid to dip heavily into magical realism especially in my collection, *Devil Talk*. And because I was raised as a Roman Catholic and converted to Judaism in adulthood, I've touched upon issues of intermarriage, religious tensions and even the Holocaust.

I saw no reason to stray from these themes. I kept reminding myself that this novel would have to be fun to write. Otherwise why do it? I didn't want to get bored with the characters or plot, something that never happens when I write short stories. I mean, look, they're short. You get in, you get out. It's a little thrill ride with no time for things to get dull.

I eventually came upon the overarching inspiration and structure for my novel that would pull together all of these elements. Maybe it wouldn't sell, but so what? (That noise you hear is my agent sighing—deeply, sadly.) But I knew that if I were to write a novel, this would be it.

I also knew that my novel would not have the panoramic, epic breadth of, say, Luis Alberto Urrea's brilliant *The Hummingbird's Daughter* (2005). It would be closer to the novel-in-stories such as one of my favorite books, *The Joy Luck Club* (1989) by Amy Tan, or perhaps Laila Lalami's exquisite *Hope and Other Dangerous Pursuits* (2005). While the chapters would connect, I wanted each to be able to stand alone as a short story, to be self-contained and a world unto itself. Not only did I want to touch on some of my favorite themes, I also hoped to address such timely topics as the quagmire in Iraq, Los Angeles politics (especially our Chicano mayor), immigration and assimilation.

Once I settled on the themes and structure, I approached each chapter with the joyful giddiness I get from starting a new short story.

That was about a year ago. I finished the novel and sent it to my agent and she, in turn, forwarded the manuscript to a couple of editors who wanted to see me make the leap to the long form. Now all we can do is wait. Will they like my novel? God only knows.

But I had a damn fun time writing it.

SC DEFEATS OREGON STATE, 21-0 (See Sports Section)

Times Telephone Numbers
• MAdison 5-2345 for subscriber service calls and all other calls except those concerning classified advertising.
• MAdison 5-4411 for all classified advertising calls.

Los Angeles Times
EQUAL RIGHTS
LIBERTY UNDER THE LAW — TRUE INDUSTRIAL FREEDOM

9 A.M. FINAL

VOL. LXXVII — IN FOUR PARTS — SATURDAY MORNING, SEPTEMBER 20, 1958 — 44 PAGES — DAILY 10c

KHRUSHCHEV WARNS U.S. OF WORLD WAR

HOW UCLA, PITT LINE UP FOR GAME

Kickoff 2 p.m. at Coliseum

PITTSBURGH No.	Name	Wt.	Pos.	Wt.	UCLA Name	No.
80	Zanos	193	LER	196	Steffen (C)	86
78	Montanari	200	LTR	216	Lecka	72
65	Guzik	223	LGR	187	Harper	63
50	Crafton (C)	190	C	200	Butler	54
62	Michaels (C)	196	RGL	206	Whitfield	64
75	Lindner	215	RTL	205	Dawson	78
83	Goh	215	REL	182	Wallen	82
19	Kaliden	187	QB	207	Gertsman	41
30	Haley	185	LHR	195	Parslow	38
36	Scisly	180	RHL	177	Long	14
45	Riddle	193	FB	193	R. Smith	21

203—Average Weight Linemen—199
187—Average Weight Backs—193
196—Average Weight Team—197

PITTSBURGH ROSTER

11 Sharockman, qb	62 Michaels, rg
14 Toncic, qb	63 Longfellow, lg
16 Prince, qb	64 Hodge, rg
19 Kalinden, qb	65 J. Guzik, lg
21 Sepsi, lh	66 Suffoletta, rg
21 Flara, lh	70 Merkovsky, rt
25 Reinhold, rh	72 Westwood, rt
28 Cox, rh	73 Velle, lt
30 Haley, lh	74 Marranca, rt
32 Clemens, rh	75 Lindner, rt
35 Plowman, rh	76 Fornadel, lt
36 Scisly, rh	78 Montanari, lt
41 Baracca, fb	79 Mills, lt
42 Cunningham, fb	80 Zanos, le
44 Morsillo, fb	81 Pullekines, le
45 Riddle, fb	83 Goh, re
46 Stark, fb	84 Walker, re
50 Crafton, c	85 Rathi, re
51 Fazio, c	88 Delfine, re
59 Lucci, c	88 Kuprok, re
60 Seaman, lg	89 Ditka, le
61 Corfield, lg	95 B. Guzik, rg

UCLA ROSTER

11 Kendall, lh	62 Cochran, lg
14 Long, lh	63 Harper, rg
17 Kilmer, lh	64 Whitfield, lg
21 R. Smith, fb	65 Metcalf, lg
22 R. Brown, fb	66 Dabov, rg
24 N. Smith, fb	67 Riskas, lg
25 Gaines, fb	70 Longo, rt
26 Wilson, fb	71 Wallace, lt
30 Peterson, qb	72 Lecka, rt
31 Davis, rh	73 Warner, lt
33 Luster, rh	76 Betts, rt
37 B. Smith, rh	77 Fagerholm, lt
38 Parslow, rh	78 Dawson, lt
41 Gertsman, qb	79 Oglesby, rt
43 Mackey, fb	81 Oglesby, rt
47 Phillips, qb	82 Wallen, le
48 Story, qb	83 Pierovich, re
50 Moor, c	84 Johnson, le
53 Baldwin, c	85 Almquist, re
54 Butler, c	86 Steffen, re-lh
57 Walters, c	87 Berry, re
59 Treat, c	88 Norris, re
61 King, rg	

New Bombing in Wilshire Area

Explosion Outside Theater

The unknown "pipe-bomber" struck again last night, according to police, planting the seventh homemade bomb to explode in the Wilshire district in the last five weeks.

The latest blast shattered the stillness of the Baldwin Hills area when it exploded outside the Baldwin Theater, 3721 S La Brea Ave., shortly before 11 p.m.

There were no injuries and damage consisted only of loosened exterior stucco at the theater.

Filled With Powder

Police said the water-pipe bomb that was filled with black powder was similar to the homemade bombs set off on two occasions last Friday in the area of 4th St. and Hudson Ave.

One of the bombs Friday was planted at a boulevard stop sign in that area while the other was set in a car at the intersection.

Three other bombs, also believed made by the same person or persons, were set off in the neighborhood earlier in the week and another exploded on a lawn there more than a month ago, officers said.

LIGHT FOR THE GENERAL—Daughter Patricia Jane lights Gen. Curtis LeMay's cigar at National Press Club's father-daughter dinner in Washington. The Air Force Vice-Chief of Staff has just returned from Far East bases tour.

Says Red China Will Fight If Yank Forces Remain on Formosa

MOSCOW, Sept. 19 (AP)—Premier Khrushchev tonight warned President Eisenhower to withdraw U.S. forces from Formosa immediately or risk their forceful expulsion by Communist China.

If the United States does not pull out its forces now, the Soviet leader said, then "no other way will be left to People's China except expulsion of armed forces hostile to it from its own territory . . ."

Khrushchev's strong letter was handed to U.S. Charge d'Affaires Richard Davis at the Soviet Foreign Ministry.

(At Newport, R.I., where he is vacationing, there was no immediate comment from President Eisenhower on the Khrushchev note.)

Western Reaction

First reaction from some western diplomats was that they did not consider Khrushchev's letter an ultimatum, but rather a reply strong enough to match a letter President Eisenhower sent Khrushchev Sept. 12.

In his letter the President called on the Soviet Union to urge Red China to renounce use of force in Formosa Strait and embark on peaceful negotiations.

A Tass Agency summary of Khrushchev's reply said the Kremlin leader again warned that an attack on Red China would be considered an attack on the Soviet Union.

Stands With China

"We stand fully by the side of the Chinese People's government and the Chinese people," Khrushchev said.

The Premier declared that "a nuclear blackmail against People's China would intimidate neither us — the U.S.S.R. — nor the People's Republic of China."

He said China would never agree with "the severance of its very own territory" nor with the existence of foreign armed forces concentrated in that area. He demanded that "interference in the internal affairs

Please Turn to Pg. 4, Col. 1

Third Smog Alert Seen for Today

A third smog alert may be declared today to follow yesterday's first-stage alert that was called at 1:08 p.m. when a bitter, yellow cloud of choking fumes sent the ozone count to .51 in Pasadena.

An alert is automatic whenever the ozone reaches .51 per 1,000,000 parts air.

The alert — in effect throughout the L.A. Basin—lasted for 37 minutes. It was called off at 1:45 p.m. when the ozone reading dropped to below .40 at all stations.

This was the second alert in as many days. The first alert since July 31, 1957, was called Thursday when the ozone reached a suffocating .53 at Pershing Square.

Another Alert

The Air Pollution Control District warned that there may be a third alert today.

The APCD forecast calls for moderate smog and weak winds in the central, southeastern and foothill areas and inland valleys.

But although the smog was heavy, temperatures failed to climb to the 94 high forecast earlier by the weatherman.

Yesterday's readings ranged from 66 at 5 a.m. to 89 at 12:27 p.m., while the humidity dropped from 57% at midnight to 32% at 12:30 p.m.

As the second alert was sounded yesterday, protests from irate citizens poured

Please Turn to Pg. 5, Col. 4

Algeria Rebels Set Up Exile Government

BY WALDO DRAKE
Times European Bureau

PARIS, Sept. 19 — An ax which has hung over France's head for two years fell today when the Moslem rebels' National Liberation Front, FLN, announced in Cairo the formation of a provisional revolutionary government in exile.

Although this action cannot provide any immediate reinforcement to rebel terrorists in Algeria it does presage FLN's determination to continue the four-year-old struggle for independence regardless of what measures for peace may be taken by Premier De Gaulle.

Named as the first Prime Minister was Ferhat Abbas, 59, a druggist from Setif, Algeria, a man long in the forefront of the Algerian rebel movement.

The exile regime in Cairo

Please Turn to Pg. 4, Col. 3

Council Defies Mayor, Puts Pay Issue on Ballot

BY CARLTON WILLIAMS

Defying the Mayor and civic leaders who asked that the measures be held over until the regular municipal elections next spring, the City Council yesterday took final action to place two city issues on the November State election ballot at a cost to city taxpayers of about $80,000.

First of these measures is a proposed City Charter amendment which, if approved by the voters, will make it much simpler for city employees to get salary boosts.

The second is a $10,000,000 Fire Department bond issue which Mayor Poulson charges was readied for the ballot only to justify the expense of submitting the salary amendment, sought by Fire and Police Protective League and the All City Employees Association.

Last Plea Made

Members of the Fire Commission made a last plea before the Council yesterday to have their bond issue removed from the ballot but

Please Turn to Pg. 5, Col. 1

U.S. Balks Red China Seat in U.N.

UNITED NATIONS, Sept. 19 (AP)—The United States won its first major test today in efforts to shelve the issue of Red China's membership in the United Nations for another year.

The victory came in the U.N.'s powerful 21-nation Steering Committee after bitter debate in which Soviet Dep. Foreign Minister Zorin accused the United States of cowardice and U.S. Ambassador Lodge charged the Soviet Union with vilifying the United States.

By a vote of 12-7 with two abstentions the committee approved a U.S. proposal to recommend to the 81-nation General Assembly that it reject at this session any proposals to exclude the Chinese Nationalists now in the U.N. or to seat representatives of Red China.

The recommendation goes to the Assembly, where the United States is confident it will be approved.

UAW Ready for Chrysler, GM Strike

DETROIT, Sept. 19 (AP) — The United Auto Workers tonight served notice they would strike General Motors and Chrysler, but held out hopes that contract settlements could be reached to avert the walkout.

UAW President Walter Reuther said the UAW international executive board authorized GM workers to strike Sept. 30. He said the Chrysler strike deadline would be selected in the light of progress made in further negotiations.

Reuther said he will enter the Chrysler-UAW talks tomorrow and said, "I think I can find out tomorrow if Chrysler wants to talk seri-

Please Turn to Pg. 5, Col. 3

U.S. Living Costs Dip First Time in 2 Years

WASHINGTON, Sept. 19 (AP)—Living costs as measured by the government dropped in August for the first time in two years. The fall was 2%.

The Labor Department attributed the decline to the usual late summer drop in food prices as fruits and vegetables hit the market in quantity.

Ewan Clague, the government's price expert, said no sustained living cost decline is in sight. He forecast the consumer price level will stay approximately where it is for the next few months.

Cost of Goods and Services Off Slightly

Los Angeles prices of goods and services followed the national trend by declining 2% in August from July, Max D. Kossoris, regional director of the Bureau of Labor Statistics, said yesterday.

The index drop from 125.4

Please Turn to Pg. 2, Col. 2

THE WEATHER

Smog today. Possible alert.

U.S. Weather Bureau forecast: Increasing night and morning fog and low clouds today and tomorrow with mostly sunny but slightly cooler days. High today near 84. Yesterday's high, 89; low, 66.

INDEX OF FEATURES

DETAILS OF $40,000 CONTEST ON PAGE 8

Details of the gigantic Road to Riches contest with prizes totaling $40,000 in cash and new cars will be found in today's Times, Page 8, Part, I.

First prize in the contest is $15,000 and a choice of a new Thunderbird, Chevrolet Impala or Plymouth station wagon. Second prize is $3500 and one of the two remaining cars and third prize is the third car and $1000.

Everyone in the family will enjoy the interesting, amusing puzzles that are to be solved. A sample is included in today's announcement.

Still-Foreign Correspondent

Tu Ciudad (2006)

"Thank you," she said as I signed the book.

"You're very welcome," I responded without looking up.

"No, really," she said. "Thank you for introducing me to a whole new world that I didn't know existed," she explained.

The middle-aged woman, who did not appear to be Latina, smiled broadly and walked away. As I continued to sign my book for the other customers, I remained puzzled by the exchange.

I've written four books: a novella, two short-story collections and one children's book. My fiction tends to center on the lives of Chicanos and other Latinos. I usually pepper my stories with a little Spanish to reflect the way my characters speak, though it's at a fairly basic level and easily understood by context. In any event, when people decide to attend one of my readings, they usually know what they're going to get.

What confused me about the woman's comment was that my stories, though reflecting my cultural experiences, nonetheless focus on universal themes such as love, family dynamics and life's struggles. In other words, I use fiction to confront the vagaries of the human condition. But here was a woman who thought that I had introduced her to a world she never knew existed.

More than anything else I do, my book appearances remind me that to many people, the "Chicano experience" is still quite exotic and unfamiliar, even in a city such as Los Angeles. Perhaps I should be surprised or even angry about this. But I can't get upset with people who make the effort to learn something new. In fact, I give them credit for taking a step many might consider difficult or even unpleasant.

But this doesn't answer my basic question: how can Chicano characters in fiction be so unfamiliar to some? Are we still so segregated as a society that even in Los Angeles, there are adults who, when exposed to Chicano culture, feel as though they're watching a National Geographic special on a newly-discovered tribe?

Perhaps I should approach this from a different angle. During the mid-1960s to the early 1970s, I attended a Roman Catholic elementary school in a predominantly Mexican neighborhood near downtown Los Angeles. Thus, my primary exposure to the "dominant" white culture came from four sources. First, most of the nuns and lay teachers were white. Second, virtually all of the literature we studied was written by people with names such as Hemingway, O'Connor and Kipling. Third, my family's favorite TV programs included *Bewitched, The Ed Sullivan Show* and *Batman*. Finally, the magazines and newspapers that came into the house were the *Los Angeles Times, Newsweek* and *Time*.

I then attended a Jesuit high school that was predominantly white. Did I suddenly feel as though I had entered a foreign country? No, not really. I joined the football team and made plenty of friends, regardless of ethnicity. And my formal education and pop culture immersion remained decidedly mainstream.

Though print and electronic media don't necessarily reflect reality, they do convey a sense of their creators' culture. Thus, the fact that I grew up in a Mexican neighborhood did not prevent me from being immersed in the dominant society. It happened so naturally and constantly that I never even noticed.

But what will it take for the opposite to occur? Chicano culture certainly can be presented by the media more widely than it is today. But we need honest representations that are free of ugly and deceitful stereotypes. How can this be done? First, Chicanos can take the financial risk and start magazines, newspapers, publishing houses, production companies and the like. Second, the mainstream media must start figuring out that it makes good business sense to rely on Chicano talent as news anchors, authors, artists, actors and film directors. Again, by going to the source, I assume the representation of Chicano culture would be more honest and accurate than what we often see.

All of these things are already happening, though much more needs to be done. But I do hold out the hope that eventually the common non-Chicano response to my fiction will be: "Thank you for telling it like it is!" That would make my day.

Exploring the Mexican American Experience
California Lawyer (2008)

We in the legal profession have grown accustomed to the idea of lawyers who also write fiction or poetry. Poet-lawyers such as Wallace Stevens and Archibald MacLeish often come to mind. And there's this fellow named John Grisham who seems to have caught on. Indeed, at least one law journal, *Legal Studies Forum* (edited by James R. Elkins, a professor at West Virginia University College of Law), is dedicated to publishing poems, short stories, and literary analysis by attorneys, so, when I started writing fiction and poetry ten years ago while working full time as a government attorney, I realized I was not alone.

But I am not just a lawyer who writes. I am a Chicano lawyer who writes. Though my activities in the legal profession sometimes make their way into my creative writing, my fiction and poetry are chiefly grounded in and informed by my experiences growing up in a predominantly Mexican American, working-class neighborhood near downtown Los Angeles. Over the years, I've had the pleasure of reading the work of others who share both my professional and cultural touchstones.

In 1998, when I started writing, I was deeply influenced by Yxta Maya Murray's 1997 novel *Locas*, centered on two young Chicanas living in the gang-ravaged Los Angeles neighborhood of Echo Park. Murray, a 1993 graduate of Stanford Law School and a professor at Loyola Law School in L.A., began writing after her clerkship with U.S. district court Judge Harry L. Hupp.

"I had always wanted to be a writer," says Murray, "but it was only when I began working on drug, racketeering, and bank-robbery cases that I got the mojo for a novel. I was spurred into action by witnessing so many men of color get sentenced to jail."

Murray, who considers herself a mixed-race Chicana (her mother is from Mexico and her father from Canada), has published four more novels since *Locas* (1997), including *The King's Gold* (2008). "In my first two novels, I deal with urban populations; in my last three, I've dealt with the question of colonialism, both historically and contemporarily," observes Murray. "I've become fascinated with the collision of [indigenous] American and European cultures in the 16th century, and how the conquest can be felt by our community today."

Similarly, novelist Michael Nava has explored this "collision" between cultures, but with the added dimension of being a gay man in modern America. Nava, whose ethnic heritage is Mexican, Yaqui, and Cajun, graduated from Stanford Law School in 1981 and now serves as a staff attorney for California Supreme Court Associate Justice Carlos R. Moreno. In 1986 Nava published the first of seven mystery novels, *The Little Death,* in which he introduced readers to Henry Rios, a gay Chicano criminal-defense lawyer. Rios confronts contemporary issues of bigotry and the ravages of AIDS as he solves gruesome murders and other crimes. Widely recognized as a groundbreaking novelist, Nava's writing was analyzed through an in-depth interview in *Spilling the Beans in Chicanolandia: Conversations with Writers and Artists* (2006) by Frederick Luis Aldama, an English professor at Ohio State University.

"It never occurred to me that the character in my books, Henry Rios, would be other than Latino or gay," asserts Nava. "In the beginning, I was more interested in his experience as a gay man, but in the later books I made a conscious effort to explore his relationship (complex and difficult though it is) to his ethnicity, primarily through his relationship to his family." Nava adds: "As a lawyer, I am a gay Latino in an overwhelmingly white and straight profession."

Interestingly, while Murray and Nava have explored ethnicity and culture through fiction, Nicolás C. Vaca has confronted such issues primarily in his well-regarded and controversial non-fiction book, *The Presumed Alliance: The Unspoken Conflict Between Latinos and Blacks and What It Means for America* (2004). Vaca has also written in a fictional style about his former immigration law practice. Many lawyers know Vaca from his non-fiction stories that have appeared in this magazine during the past decade, including "El Borrachito" and "Burnt Beans." Over the years, I've enjoyed Vaca's stories and appreciate his poignant writing about Chicano and Mexican lives.

A graduate of Harvard Law School and a partner in the San Jose office of Garcia, Calderón & Ruíz, Vaca became a lawyer "to have an impact on society." But he started writing creatively as an undergraduate student at UC Berkeley, when he took a course on Russian literature and read Anton Chekhov, Nikolai Gogol, Ivan Turgenev, Ivan Goncharov, and others. Chekhov particularly impressed Vaca because of his "lack of idealization of the peasant class, in that he wrote about them with all their imperfections."

"In one of my midterm examinations," remembers Vaca, "I took liberty with one of the questions and answered it by trying to emulate Chekhov's writing. The professor, a Russian émigré, wrote some very nice things about my answer, and that inspired me to try to actually write short stories."

Murray, Nava, and Vaca have advice for lawyers who want to become writers: "A page a day," counsels Murray. Nava advises, "Find a writing group to encourage you, and keep the creative side of your brain active." Vaca offers tough love: "Writers write. In other words, do not call yourself a writer if you do not write on a daily basis."

Julia Sylva seems to have internalized these admonitions. A former partner at such law firms as Ochoa & Sillas and Frandzel & Share in Los Angeles, Sylva now runs her own practice in L.A. Though she has published many articles on such legal topics as the Brown Act, redevelopment law, and public finance, Sylva also "finds time to write creatively as an extracurricular activity—a challenging task for a working mom."

"I am currently drafting my memoirs," says Sylva, whose résumé includes a four-year term on the city council of Hawaiian Gardens (1976-80) in the southeast part of Los Angeles County. Through election by her colleagues, she simultaneously served two consecutive one-year terms as mayor of the town when she was in her early twenties. Then in 1979, at age 23, Sylva began attending Loyola Law School. She did not run for reelection to the city council because the dean gave her a choice: continue her legal studies on a scholarship, or seek a second term on the council. Sylva chose law over politics: "I believe I made the right choice," she says.

Aside from writing her memoirs, Sylva also has aspirations of publishing a cookbook on Mexican and Jewish cuisine, to be entitled *Kosher Tamales*. "It will include my mother's childhood recipes," she says, "and recipes we have jointly created since I converted to Judaism."

What kind of reaction should Sylva expect from her colleagues when she publishes her first book? If it's anything similar to what Nava experienced, Sylva may be pleasantly surprised. "Many of my lawyer friends through the years have been frustrated writers themselves," says Nava. "So they have been keenly interested in how I managed to do both." Murray says Loyola Law School, where she has been teaching for thirteen years, is "beyond supportive" of her writing. Conversely, Vaca wryly notes: "Most [lawyers] are only mildly impressed that I am a published writer."

But I dare say these lawyers do not write to impress their fellow attorneys. Rather, each is driven to explore through prose the intricacies, conflicts, and richness of their cultural experiences. For that, we as readers can count ourselves lucky.

A Pocho in West Hills

The Raven Chronicles (2005)

Uno: Cada uno extiende la pierna hasta donde alcanza la cubierta.
One: Each person stretches his leg as far as the cover will allow.

I'm writing this longhand because Ben, our eleven-year-old son, has yet again commandeered our sole computer to tap out a book report on *Flowers for Algernon* (1966) by Daniel Keyes. I admit that I've never read the book. He's just finished reading my wife's battered copy that she read over 30 years ago when she was about Ben's age. But I do remember seeing the movie on TV long ago, maybe when I, too, was a pre-teen. Cliff Robertson plays Charlie Gordon, the man with the mind of a young boy, who through the marvels of modern medicine, becomes a certified genius, as Wile E. Coyote is want to say as he impresses himself with his brilliant plans based on the Acme Co.'s Rube Goldberg-like, Roadrunner-catching contraptions. At the height of his mental powers (I mean Charlie's, not Wile E.'s), he both delights and confounds the medical researchers by doing everything from blithely explaining Einstein's theory of relativity to effortlessly learning dozens of living *and* dead languages. I'm sitting at our breakfast table, rain clouds threatening to soak the surrounding hills this Saturday afternoon, Bobby McFerrin's malleable, playful voice bouncing on public radio, my 43rd birthday looming but two days away, and it is the fictional Charlie's astonishing language skills that command my attention.

Dos: Las cosas hablando se entienden.
Two: Things become clear through communication.

My wife's yellowed, dog-eared high school Spanish dictionary merely defines "pocho" as a Mexican born in the United States. My equally decrepit *Cassell's* makes no mention of Mexicans or this country. Its entry is a bit more disturbing, actually. To *Cassell's*, the word signifies something that is discolored or rotten. *Rotten.* Not a nice definition. Notably, my spanking new, gift-from-my-beautiful-and-brilliant wife, *The New Shorter Oxford English Dictionary* (yes, that *is* the title of this two volume version of the stout, and unwieldy, OED) pulls together both definitions rather nicely and adds that a pocho is a "culturally Americanized Mexican." Cheers!

Tres: El que mucho habla, poco logra.
Three: He who talks much accomplishes little.

Rotten: moth-eaten, worm-eaten; mildewed, rusty, moldy, spotted, seedy, time-worn, moss-grown; discolored; effete, wasted, crumbling, moldering, cankered, blighted, tainted; depraved, decrepit; broke, busted, broken, out of commission, *hors de combat*, out of action, broken down; done, done for, done up; worn out, used up, finished; beyond saving, fit for the dust hole, fit for the wastepaper basket, past work. *¡Gracias, Roget's!*

Cuatro: Cada chango a su mecate.
Four: Each monkey to his own rope or each person to his position in life.

Ah! Ben has vacated the computer room and now my fingers dance happily across the keyboard as Susana Baca croons "De los amores" from my Labtec speakers. Where was I? Oh, yes. Pocho. When I started writing short stories a few years ago, I wrote a piece that was more a string of memories about my childhood. My story reads in pertinent part:

> When I was born, Mom and Pop decided that they would raise me in both English and Spanish with an emphasis on English.
> "Without good English, he'll never get anywhere in this world," I remember Pop saying on many occasions and I know that Mom fully agreed. So, they decided that Pop would speak only Spanish and Mom only English. At first, I favored English because I was very close to Mom as are most young boys. I know this now that I have a son. But I eventually spoke more and more Spanish particularly because Pop and I often went out together—"Just the boys," said Mom—to play ball in the street outside our home or to go to the park. When I turned three, however, I stopped speaking completely. No English. No Spanish. Mom and Pop panicked. Had they done something wrong? Did they ruin my future?
> They took me to be tested. I remember going to some kind of hospital with long cold hallways. My parents met a nice, tall man who wore a white doctor's coat and who asked them many questions. Tall bookshelves groaned under the weight of large, broad-spined medical books while dozens of stuffed animals sat helter-skelter in one, soft pile on a large, blue plastic toy box in the corner. I ran to the toys and grabbed armfuls of the plush creatures. Every so often, I would look up and catch the doctor looking at me as he explained something to my parents. The doctor was very thin with blonde hair and pale skin that made his black-rimmed glasses the most prominent feature on his face. His smiled gently. I remember wondering what was going to happen to me.
> After Mom and Pop finished answering all of the doctor's questions, the doctor led me into a small room that had a large mirror covering one wall. At the far end stood a gray table with many little colorful toys scattered on its surface. Two chairs sat

side-by-side on one side of the table. Mom was nervous about the whole process so she sat alone in the waiting room and Pop came in with me. The door closed and I sat on my hands so that I wouldn't be tempted to play with the wonderful toys that lay before me. I knew my manners even though I wasn't speaking. I then stared at the mirror and could see moving shadows behind it. Who lived back there? I thought. I figured that I should be friendly so I waved to the mirror. The shadows stopped moving. Suddenly, a sharp, metallic voice cracked the silence. My eyes jumped to a little box that hung sadly from one corner of the high ceiling.

"Hello, Joe," the voice said. It sounded like the nice doctor.

"Say 'hello,' Joe," said Pop.

I didn't answer but I smiled up at the talking box.

"We're going to ask you to do a few things with those toys. Does that sound fun, Joe?"

It sounded great to me. I grinned.

"Okay," said the voice, "Pick up the red chair and put it on the blue car."

I remember looking at the toys in front of me. What a stupid thing to ask, I thought. This is not fun. But I kept on grinning and followed the voice's directions hoping that things would improve.

"Now," continued the voice. "Put the green cowboy on the white horse," and I did it.

This "game" went on for about twenty minutes and I never made a mistake but I grew very bored. Pop rubbed my back when the voice finally said: "Okay, Joe, we're done playing with the toys. You did great."

Playing? I thought. Is this how white people play? How boring! The door creaked opened and the doctor led us to another room for another "game" this time with a woman who held a little stop watch and timed me as I did various tasks with pegs and blocks. The doctor came in the room every so often and looked at the woman's notes. Another hour passed and I think that I did very well but I was not having very much fun.

After a few more tests, the doctor came back and asked me and my parents to wait in a room down the hall. We sat in there for what seemed like hours. I looked at my parents. Pop nervously flipped through pages of a *Life* magazine and Mom stared straight ahead at nothing in particular. What was wrong? I thought. I don't like this place. Finally, the doctor came to the waiting room. He was smiling.

"Well, he's intelligent and his hearing is fine."

Mom and Pop let out a sigh at the same time.

"We have a recommendation, however. He's clearly getting confused between Spanish and English and his brain just sort of decided to shut down in terms of speaking." The doctor rubbed his eyes without removing his glasses by sliding his thumb and index finger under the rims. He looked tired.

He continued: "We recommend that you stop speaking Spanish to him. He'll eventually start talking again."

Pop's eyes grew wide. "Must we?" he asked hoping for a different remedy.

"That's our recommendation."

They followed the kind doctor's prescription for my muteness and cut all Spanish in the house. Eventually, after a year, I started speaking again, in English, and my parents' fears disappeared. In fact, Pop started calling me "motor mouth" because I talked incessantly probably to make up for lost time. I was going to do just fine in the Anglo world....

That's the beauty of fictionalizing one's life. I can insert dialogue that I surely can't remember, and I can offer unerring, lucid descriptions of the people, places and things, as well. But you get the point. Pocho. That's how that word became part of me.

Cinco: La vida no retoña.
Five: We have but one life to live.

I am the grandson of Mexican immigrants who settled in Los Angeles over 80 years ago. All of my grandparents are now gone but I only knew one, Isabel, my mother's mother. The others had died young: both grandfathers at 50 and my father's mother at 35. Isabel (after whom my own mother is named) was our strongest link to Mexico. She came from Ocotlán, Jalisco, where many of her family members still live, doing quite well with money made from ranching and then, on top of that, interstate trucking. Isabel's husband, Daniel, died a month or so before I was born. I took his name and, for that reason, I believe I had a special bond with my grandmother. Indeed, I wrote my first poem as an adult in her honor. I saw an ad in *Poets & Writers* magazine seeking poetry submissions by Latinos honoring mothers and grandmothers. The poem tumbled out of me and I submitted it to Lee & Low Books. Pat Mora, as guest editor for this project, accepted my work many months later. It appeared as one of thirteen pieces in a children's picture book, *Love to Mamá: A Tribute to Mothers* (2001). The poem, entitled "Hidden in Abuelita's Soft Arms," reads:

Wrinkled and brown like an old paper bag,
Abuelita smiles with her too-perfect white teeth,
And she calls out as I run from Papa's old, gray station wagon,
"Mi cielo, come here! I need a big abrazo from you!"

And I bury myself deep, hidden in Abuelita's soft arms,
Smelling like perfume and frijoles and coffee and candy.

A whole weekend with Abuelita!
I shout, "Bye, Papa!"

Papa smiles and drives off in a puff of white smoke.
I bury my face deeper into her,
Just me and Abuelita,
For the whole weekend.

We march happily into her house
Painted yellow-white like a forgotten Easter egg,
And cracked here and there like that same egg.
But it is her home,
Near the freeway and St. Agnes Church.

On the wall there are pictures of Mama and my two aunts.
And there's one of Abuelita, so young and beautiful,
Standing close to Abuelito on their wedding day.

"Mi cielo," Abuelita says holding my sweaty cheeks in her
Cool, smooth hands.
"You are so big! My big boy!"
And I laugh and stand on my toes to be even bigger.

And I bury myself deep, hidden in Abuelita's soft arms,
Smelling like perfume and frijoles and coffee and candy.

I wonder what my grandmother would have thought of my
writing. I suppose it really doesn't matter. I enjoyed her so much
while she was here, and now I can bring her to others in my poems
and stories.

Seis: Las cosas hablando se entienden (otra vez).
Six: Things become clear through communication (again).

I try my best to use Spanish in my fiction and poetry despite my
struggles with the language. I've collected wonderful Spanish
reference books that help me in this endeavor. Why do I bother?
Well, perhaps I'm ceaselessly attempting to make up for my
deficiency, my status as a pocho. That's the psychology of it, I
suppose. Artistically, I populate my stories and poems with people I
knew while growing up the working-class, Mexican community
sandwiched between Koreatown to the north, and Pico-Union to the
east a few miles from downtown Los Angeles. They used a blended
Spanish—Spanglish or pochismos—in their everyday speech. Thus, if

I am to paint a true world in my writing, I have to make my characters speak like real people. At first I hesitated doing so. As a litigator, the only foreign language that ever seeped into my writing included such terms as *respondeat superior, res judicata, inter alia*, and other Latin terms. What would non-Chicanos think of my stories if I peppered them with another tongue? My answer came in the form of an e-mail one day a few years ago. I had finished a short story and posted it on the Zoetrope writers' workshop Web page. A non-Latino writer offered some very kind words for my story but had one major criticism: I didn't use *enough* Spanish. Apparently, she liked my use of the language in the early part of the story, but she noticed that it seemed to taper off as the story progressed. She wanted more! She thought it added a wonderful flavor to the dialogue. As far as I was concerned, this ended my internal debate. Spanish belonged in my writing. Period.

Siete: Hijo de tigre, tigrillo.
Seven: Son of a tiger, baby tiger.

One drab winter day, my son and I walked through the Topanga Plaza towards the food court chatting about his friends, homework and other such things. Suddenly, a person called to us. We looked up and saw a young woman standing by a kiosk equipped with two computer screens. She asked if we wanted to partake in a consumer survey and win a free gift. My son, who is a sucker for free gifts of any value, said, "Sure!" She directed Ben to read the questions displayed on one of the computers and choose whatever answers he wanted by touching the correct spot on the screen, so he diligently went through questions about soft drinks, tennis shoes, clothing, fast food, etc. When he came to the final screen, he had to identify himself by age, gender and ethnicity. With respect to the last category, the choices included White, Asian, Black, Native American, Hispanic and "other." He paused for a moment and thought. I thought, too. My wife is of Russian-Jewish descent and I converted to Judaism in 1988. Our son is a beautiful blend of both of us and is very proud of his mixed heritage. But what would he choose? Eventually, he smiled and whispered, "Hispanic" as he made his choice. The young woman returned the smile and offered him a choice of little prizes. Ben chose a padded CD case. We said our thanks and continued our trek to the food court.

"Isn't this cool, Papa?" he asked as he held up the black and silver CD case.

I smiled. "Yes," I said without looking at the prize. "Yes, mijo. This is cool."

Ocho: El que la sigue la consige.
Eight: He who pursues it will get it.

One week has passed since I started writing this piece. The weather has turned hot—San Fernando Valley hot—and Ben swims in our pool as I read his teacher's comments on the *Flowers for Algernon* book report. Grade: A. The teacher's red ink spills out praise for Ben's understanding of the book and use of language to describe his thoughts. The last page of the report is a mock letter Ben wrote to the author. The final sentence reads: "Thank you, Daniel Keyes, for inspiring me, and hopefully inspiring many others, because the more people treat others with respect and kindness, the better this world will become." A beautiful sentence. A beautiful sentiment. ¿No?

Cuento de Fantasma

The Elegant Variation (2005)

A few years ago, I read the following call for submissions for short stories by Mexican American writers:

> *Written in the spirit of the cuento de fantasma, the stories should include some element of folklore, superstition, religion, myth, or history. This supernatural element may be subtle or it may be prominent in the story. I am not looking for simple retellings of folktales or ghost stories, but I am interested in reinterpretations of such tales, particularly if they are placed in a contemporary setting.*

The "I" in the call for submissions was (and still is) Rob Johnson, associate professor of English at the University of Texas-Pan American University. It seems that Johnson got the idea for the anthology when he was teaching a creative writing class in 1996 and asked the students to take a folktale and retell it as a contemporary short story. What he got back from his students, many of whom were Mexican American, surprised and confused him. He read wonderfully strange stories based on traditional Mexican legends spun with modern-day jargon and sensibilities. Were these simply ghost stories and urban legends or was he being exposed to a "specific kind of typical writing?"

I'll return to Johnson's query shortly...back to that call for submissions. I had been writing short fiction for about two years when I saw Johnson's ad. At that point, I had produced about twenty or so short stories most of which were based on my experiences as a Chicano growing up in a working class neighborhood near downtown Los Angeles. But I had also produced a few oddballs. These stories sometimes mixed ancient Aztec gods with modern Christian entities, or simply offered a bizarre other-reality as a given. I blended contemporary slang and sentiment recklessly with traditional Mexican concepts of good and evil. A couple of print and online journals published these strange, hybrid tales including one entitled, "Don de la Cruz and the Devil of Malibu" which Andrei Codrescu published in the online literary journal, *Exquisite Corpse*.

Well, I had a little story, "The Plumed Serpent of Los Angeles," that I figured fit Johnson's call for submissions. I sent it in and, happily, Johnson accepted it. The final result was *Fantasmas: Supernatural Stories by Mexican American Writers*, published in 2000 by Arizona State University's Bilingual Press. The anthology includes stories by twenty writers including Kathleen Alcalá, David Rice, Stephen D. Gutiérrez and Elva Treviño Hart. Now back to Johnson's musings. In his foreword to the anthology, Johnson observes that the cuento de fantasma has its roots with the magical realists such as Jorge Luis Borges, Gabriel García Máquez and Julio Cortázar. But there was something else happening with the modern stories included in his anthology: a belief that the supernatural is a part of reality, not separate from it. Further, he saw issues of race and class addressed under cover of spirits, el Diablo and ancient gods.

In the anthology's introduction, novelist/short story writer Kathleen Alcalá asserts that cuentos de fantasma serve "as a bridge between traditional storytelling and pulp fiction, incorporating elements of both." Alcalá identifies four elements common to these stories: (1) basis in oral tradition; (2) influence of folk religions; (3) use of vernacular forms; and (4) influence of life and culture from the United States side of the border. She also notes that the fantasma "has been used as a vehicle for conveying political and social truths that could be fatal if presented more baldly." Thus, dictators "have been transformed into packing shed bosses, abusive husbands, and the turbulent desires of the heart."

Though my contribution to the *Fantasma* anthology could have been written without any fear of governmental retribution, the "roots" of the story are clearly embedded with the tradition Alcalá and Johnson have identified. "The Plumed Serpent of Los Angeles" (which first appeared in the online journal *Southern Cross Review* before ending up in the anthology) does address issues of European conquests and the imposition of foreign belief systems on indigenous people. But it does so with humor, allowing ancient Aztec gods to wrangle with the Christian god of evil, the Devil (here la Diabla, the female version of that entity). Thus, if I lived in a totalitarian regime where the government feared the expression of contrary political sentiments (no knowing chuckling, folks), my use of the fantasma form would likely protect my message from being used against me in a kangaroo court.

But not all cuentos de fantasma need to be political. For example, in my story "Monk" (which was accepted and edited by the remarkable writer James Sallis for the online journal *In Posse Review*), I tell the tale of one man's midlife crisis as he confronts the expectations of his parents and his assumed expectations of his much younger girlfriend. A recurring element in the story is the protagonist's dream life. Sallis introduces the story with this observation: "We live our lives ever divided: tangible reality of the world outside us, our perception of the world. It's at the juncture—at the collision of that world and our inmost attempts to explain it to ourselves, i.e., our fantasies—that our personalities are formed and our destinies defined."

Heady stuff. But Sallis correctly describes the essence of the story which is in line with the commentary of both Johnson and Alcalá. "Monk" is included in my most recent collection, *Devil Talk* (2004). In a review published by the *El Paso Times*, poet and novelist Rigoberto González says: "In a stunning departure from the social realism of his previous collection...Olivas takes readers into a disarming otherworld of the surreal and the supernatural.... The quick succession of 26 narratives covers a wide territory of moods, from the strangely elliptical to the whimsical."

Though the review certainly delighted me, I was startled by the description. I considered the stories to be fun, a little different, sometimes a bit dark. But I think that the cuento de fantasma form lends itself such a response. When you mix the supernatural with reality as freely as you mix a martini, the results could be just as intoxicating.

Great Expectations
LatinoLA (2004)

All right, you should know up front that I do not intend to whine about the alleged suffering and wretchedness of a writer trying to sell his wares at a well-planned book signing in a major bookstore nestled near the food court of an immense Southern California mall. First, I make my living as a government lawyer so I don't need the $1.10 I make off of every sale of my short-story collection. Second, I'm a father of a thirteen-year-old boy so I know from suffering and wretchedness (mostly mine, sometimes his). Third, I write fiction because I must; I have no choice, so selling the final product is not the ends; it is merely an unfortunate byproduct.

Okay, that said, I have a secret: despite being an attorney, I am also a human being. Yes, it's true, and as with most human beings, I want to be liked. And if a person buys one of my books directly from me, it's as if that customer is saying: "I like you. You are a good person." So, as they say, I've shown you all my cards, right? Let's move on.

I've done book signings before, and this one shouldn't be any different. Except I have seen how signings work at this particular bookstore. There is no room for readings so it is strictly meet-greet-sell-sign. I've wandered past the forlorn authors sitting at the black-draped table just outside the bookstore's wide corner entrance. I've witnessed people steer their course around these poor, abandoned writers so as to avoid eye-contact because acknowledgment means a potential obligation to stop and perhaps buy the latest book on terriers or winter baking, and I admit that I've done the same thing to avoid these suffering artists.

My signing would be different. Bilingual Press, my publisher, has touted me as a "rising voice in Chicano fiction" (it must be true: it says so on the back of my book). My book has just received a glowing review from a large Texas newspaper. I had this brilliant piece of Lone Star writing blown-up and turned into a mini-poster for my signing table. The *Los Angeles Times* Sunday book section and *LatinoLA* had published notices heralding my upcoming signing (well, heralding might be an exaggeration). Dozens of e-mails flew from my computer through cyberspace to numerous family members, friends and colleagues. The bookstore had ordered a couple dozen copies for the signing. Latino fiction is hot. Right? Those books would sell out in two seconds! I planned to bring along several copies to appease the literary mob that surely would be grateful for my planning ahead.

I arrive a half an hour before the noon signing. Ah! A beautiful, large poster proclaims my four-hour appearance. The assistant manager, a young woman who is all smiles and nods, helps me set up. "Good luck!" she chirps. I like her a lot right then. She loves books and she wants me to do well. God bless her!

I set up my table perfectly: the blow-up of the Texas book review to my left near a standing copy of my book. In the middle stands neat little stacks of my book. I also set out about a twenty copies of the book review and a little bowl of leftover Halloween candy as a special treat for my soon-to-be customers. Just in case there's a lull in the literary festivities, I have a couple of writers' magazines to keep me busy. Okay, readers of Los Angeles, I'm ready for you!

Hour one: So far, the Halloween candy is the biggest hit. Two adorable tikes run up and ask if they can have a treat. I smile at the well-behaved children. I look up at their parents who quickly turn away to avoid making eye contact. "Yes, of course," I say to the children. "Take two." Their parents say come along and they all disappear into the food court. As they leave, I hear one of the children ask, "He was a nice man, wasn't he?" They've moved too far for me to hear the answer.

Hour two: Okay, things are a bit better. Several people have actually spoken to me but I haven't sold a book yet. But I learn a trick: if I look up from my magazine before potential customers are ready to make human contact, they scurry away, so, like a fisherman, I have to be patient. Don't reel them in too soon. Let them come close, get hooked by the book's cover, the glowing review, my gentle visage. Though I sell no books two hours in, I have encouraged several people to take a copy of the book review and think it over. They all react the same way: they smile and look grateful that I've given them permission to walk away.

Then one customer wearing a grin the size of the San Fernando Valley walks up to me.

"You wrote this book?" the slightly disheveled, 30-something smiling man says. He's carrying a fresh, new bag from one of the department stores so he must have disposable income.

"Yes," I say. "My first short-story collection."

"I want someone to write my story," he offers, still grinning. "I've been abused by society."

What do I say? This poor soul is hurting. "Maybe you should write it," I finally offer. "It would be cathartic."

"Yes," he says. "That's what people tell me."

He asks the price (very reasonable he opines) and says that he's going to browse in the bookstore and then come back to buy a copy. I never see him again.

A very thin, well-tanned, un-smiling middle-aged woman comes up to fill the void and says, "You wrote a book."

I smile.

"Someone should write my life story," she continues.

"Oh?" I say.

"My divorce alone would make a great book."

I offer the same suggestion as I did to the grinning man. She nods and takes a book review. She leaves without opening her purse.

Hour three: One of the young sales women comes by to see how I'm doing. Kind of slow, I say. She smiles and buys a copy for her mother. I want to kiss her feet right there and then.

Hour four: "There you are!"

I look up from an article about how to have a successful book signing and see an old friend of mine and her teenage daughter.

"Dante!" I almost squeal. I get up and we hug. Her daughter runs into the bookstore because she's a big reader. Dante, a brilliant lawyer who used to work in my office, buys three copies. THREE COPIES! One for herself and her husband, one for a cousin and one for her mother. I sign all three with my very best penmanship. Things will pick up now! After a few more minutes of pleasant chat, her daughter emerges from the bookstore and we say our good-byes. I feel very liked.

Then another person comes to my table and he buys a book! Then several others come up and another book sells. I need to start packing up, but I don't want to lose any potential customers so I stay a half-hour past my scheduled time. Several people are now gathered about my table discussing race relations, the recent recall election, and immigration policy. They don't end up buying but they all take copies of the book review and ask if they can come by later in the week. Yes, of course. There will be autographed copies waiting.

The assistant manager thanks me and says that it was a good day. She's sure people with book reviews in hand will make it back to the bookstore and buy. She is a saint.

I get home and my wife asks how it went. I give her a big hug and kiss.

"Great," I say. "Let's get dinner. I'm hungry."

My son perks up. "Yeah," he says as he grabs his jacket. "I'm starved. Let's eat at the mall."

We jump into the car and head to the building where I had just spent five hours signing six books. As we drive, I make my wife and son laugh with stories of my recent literary adventures. I am a very lucky writer. I'm an even luckier human being.

Czech Teen's Words and Art Put a
Face on the Holocaust for Me
Jewish Journal (2007)

I attended grades one through eight at St. Thomas the Apostle School in Los Angeles during a time of great unrest in our country—the Vietnam War, the assassinations of Robert Kennedy and Dr. Martin Luther King, Jr., police brutality against war protestors during the Chicano Moratorium. Yet one of my strongest memories is reading excerpts from Anne Frank's diary. I remember being moved by the words of that remarkable little Jewish girl with large eyes who hid from the Nazis for two years. I also remember the horror of learning that the Nazis eventually found Anne and her family and that she died in a typhus epidemic that ran through the Bergen-Belsen concentration camp. Anne's diary spoke to this Los Angeles classroom across the decades, across an ocean, across cultures, across religions.

That little Chicano boy never could have imagined that someday he would grow up and fall in love with a Jewish woman, marry in a temple, convert to Judaism and send his son to a Jewish day school for eight years.

But what did Anne Frank's story offer me and my classmates at that time? The nuns who set the curriculum knew. While it is pretty near impossible to comprehend the annihilation of millions, Anne Frank offered us a face, one child to whom we could relate. Of course the questions came. Who would want to kill this little girl? Will it happen again? Could it happen to us?

Atlantic Monthly Press now brings us the English translation of *The Diary of Petr Ginz: 1941 - 1942* (2007) which, as with Anne Frank's diary, puts a face on the Holocaust through the words and artwork of a precocious teenager. Simply put, this book should be read by everyone.

Petr was a Czech Jew, born in 1928, and who died in a gas chamber in Auschwitz at the age of sixteen. His diary had been lost for 60 years but resurfaced in 2003. Petr's sister, Chava Pressburger, edited her older brother's diary entries which cover the eleven months before Petr's deportation from Prague to the Theresienstadt concentration camp. Also included are poems, an excerpt from one of Petr's unfinished novels, articles from Vedem (a weekly magazine Petr started in Theresienstadt), as well as linocuts, sketches and watercolor paintings. There is little doubt that if Petr had survived, he would have developed into an accomplished writer and artist.

Petr's entries recount the daily routine of a teenager attending school and spending time with friends and family. But interspersed amongst the quotidian details are observations that illustrate the tightening Nazi noose: "In the morning I did my homework. Otherwise nothing special. Actually, a lot is happening, but it is not even visible. What is quite ordinary now would certainly cause upset in a normal time. For example, Jews don't have fruit, geese, and any poultry, cheese, onions, garlic, and many other things. Tobacco ration cards are forbidden to prisoners, madmen, and Jews."

There are poems with lines such as these: "Today it's clear to everyone / who is a Jew and who's an Aryan, / because you'll know Jews near and far / by their black and yellow star."

Yet, despite all this, Petr loved to play pranks and possessed a wicked sense of humor as shown by this observation written on April 20, 1942: "Every building has to hang out a swastika flag, except for the Jews, of course, who are not allowed this pleasure."

Aside from his writings, Petr's artwork is noteworthy for its detail and sophistication. There is an eerie 1943 watercolor entitled "Ghetto Dwellings" that captures a foreboding atmosphere that would be difficult to replicate in words.

Petr had a particular love for the linocut which requires great control over the tools needed to carve images into small pieces of linoleum, a process similar to making woodcuts. In one of his Vedem articles, Petr describes this art form: "As the entire linocut technique shows, a linocut is the expression of a person who does not make compromises. It is either black or white. There is no grey transition."

In another Vedem piece, Petr explains that even in the squalor and deprivation of the Theresienstadt concentration camp, creativity can thrive: "The seed of a creative idea does not die in mud and scum. Even there it will germinate and spread its blossom like a star shining in the darkness." Petr proved this to be true as he founded a magazine and continued to write and create artwork while in the camp.

Also included in this book are photographs of Petr and his family. There is one from February 1933 of Petr and Chava holding hands, walking toward to the camera, both dressed in thick coats, knitted caps and scarves to protect them from the Prague winter. The five-year-old Petr has a determined look in his eyes, lips tight with purpose, as he leads his younger sister along the city street. Petr's face is the face of all children whose lives were cut short by the Nazis, and it is a face that implores us to remember two essential words: Never again.

THE COURTSHIP OF
MARIA RIVERA PENA

A NOVELLA BY
DANIEL A. OLIVAS

My Second Act as a Writer
Daily Journal (2010)

Ten years ago, at the age of 41, I did something that forever changed the trajectory of my personal life.

No, I did not leave my brilliant, beautiful wife, nor did I abandon my legal career with the California Department of Justice.

Ten years ago, I published my first book, *The Courtship of María Rivera Peña* (2000), a novella loosely based on my paternal grandparents' migration from Mexico to Los Angeles in the late 1920s. It garnered a few nice reviews, but didn't sell many copies, and the small Pennsylvania press that published it eventually went under so that the book has now gone out of print.

Here it is, ten years later, and I'm still a government lawyer married to my law school sweetheart. Our son is in college and becoming a fine, interesting young man. But my first little book put me on a road to something so exciting and emotionally fulfilling that it holds a special place in my heart.

That road has taken me to the publication of three short-story collections and one children's picture book. My fiction, poetry, and creative non-fiction appear in eight anthologies, including in two published by the venerable W. W. Norton & Co. Next year, the University of Arizona Press will publish my first full-length novel, *The Book of Want*. I've also become a recognized book critic for several publications including the *El Paso Times*, the *MultiCultural Review*, and a nationally-recognized blog on Latino literature, *La Bloga*. My books have been studied by undergraduate and graduate students across the country at such institutions as Rutgers, Ohio State University, the University of Wyoming, and the University of California, Irvine, to name a few. Scholars cite to my fiction and interviews in books on Latino literature. I've edited a landmark anthology of Latino fiction, *Latinos in Lotusland* (2008), and my first poetry collection is making the rounds with publishers.

In short, my second act has cast me as a writer.

On many levels, this second act has come along with a bit of irony. When I majored in English at Stanford University (back when my hair was long and we danced to the Bee Gees), I had no intention of doing something as risky as "becoming a writer." In fact, I purposely avoided taking any creative writing classes because I thought that it would be a frivolous thing to do, so I went to law school, spent a few years in private practice, and then in 1990, I was hired into the Public Rights Division of the California Department of Justice. I've been there ever since.

But I always loved writing. As a law student at UCLA, I edited the *Chicano Law Review* and published a piece on an important immigration court decision. As an attorney, I've written many articles for the *Los Angeles Daily Journal* on such subjects as civil procedure, law and motion practice, and environmental enforcement, and, of course, every day at work, I write briefs, legal memoranda, and letters to opposing counsel. The written word filled my world.

Then, in late 1998, I started that first little book, a novella based on family history. I wrote about the great joys and sadness in life and explored what the immigrant experience must have felt like for people such as my grandparents who came to California from Mexico almost a hundred years ago. When I completed the novella in 1999 and sold it to a little press in Pennsylvania, the creative writing floodgates opened. I couldn't stop writing fiction. As my short stories started getting published in literary journals, I began to dabble in poetry, and then book reviews.

I'm certainly not the first attorney to write fiction. We all know about Scott Turow and John Grisham. But there are also Latino and Latina lawyers who have made their mark as writers such as Michael Nava, Yxta Maya Murray, and Nicolás Vaca, to name but a few who live and write in California. These attorneys all have excelled in the legal profession yet they also have been recognized for their evocative and often provocative books that explore the Latino experience from decidedly different angles.

My "other life" has led me to experiences that have been markedly different from my life as a lawyer. I've read fiction and poetry at high schools, colleges, bookstores and scholarly conferences. This has introduced me to lovers of literature, which by itself, would be enough to validate my second act.

But I've also had high school and college students, many of whom are Latino, come up to me after readings and tell me that they want to write. These bright, eager young people see my second act as something they want to do as their first act. My response is always the same: If you want to become a writer, stay in school and read, read, read.

I don't regret waiting until middle age to become a writer. In many ways, I think my fiction and poetry are deeper and richer because I've lived more than a few years as a husband, father and (yes) lawyer.

I admit that my second act has been a surprise to me, my family and my friends. But I've learned that life can be surprising. Who knows? Maybe there's a third act in my future.

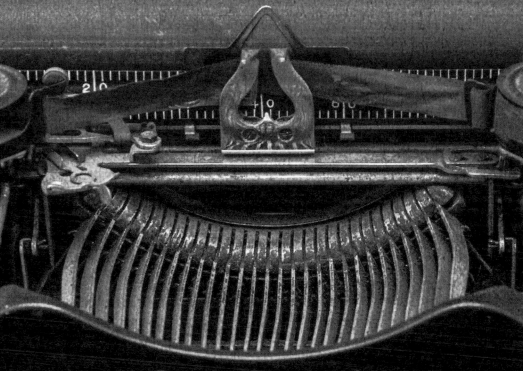

Writers Write. Period.

La Bloga (2006)

When I hear would-be authors proclaim that they could write the Great American Novel if only they had time, I simply want to laugh. It reminds me of the story (perhaps apocryphal) about a dentist who blithely informed Isabel Allende that he planned to become a novelist when he retired. She quipped: "Oh really? When I retire I'll become an oral surgeon!"

What I'm about to say will sound like tough love or even cruel, but here goes: A writer finds time to write regardless of hectic schedules, energetic children, and needy lovers. No excuses.

Rather than leave it at that, let me describe how I've written five books (four published, one making the rounds awaiting judgment), edited a 115,000-word anthology of short fiction set for publication next year, in addition to posting each Monday on *La Bloga*, and writing book reviews and essays for numerous print and online publications. I do this while juggling the time demands of marriage, parenthood and holding down a stressful, full-time day job as an attorney with the California Department of Justice.

First, I note that as a lawyer, I essentially write for a living. Though some time is spent in court, most of the "heavy lifting" occurs in my office at my computer as I write legal memoranda, motions and briefs. I work under tight, court-determined deadlines. There is no room for writers' block. My goal with legal writing is simply to tell a coherent, compelling story, so if you have a "day job" where you must write, you have an advantage that other budding authors don't because you are constantly honing your writing skills. True, writing a memo to your boss on how to improve sales might not resemble that detective thriller brewing in your brain, but I truly believe that being required, on a daily basis, to craft sentences and paragraphs in a non-literary forum will benefit your creative writing.

Second, I specialize in short stories. Even the novel I'm working on is made up of interconnecting short stories. In other words, I write self-contained pieces that I can complete within a relatively short period. This works for me. But if you want to write a novel and you feel as though you can barely get an hour alone at the computer, let me suggest that you break it up into baby steps so that the mountain you're about to scale doesn't seem so daunting. Promise yourself to write 500 words a day. That's two, double-spaced pages. Not so scary, right? I write in the evening, usually when my son is asleep and my wife is relaxing. I find that I can squeeze in one or two hours of writing each night. On weekends, I'll sneak in another one or two hours in the morning. Those hours add up as do the pages.

Third, I don't waste my time talking about what I want to write. Don't get me wrong. I love discussing the craft itself when I'm in the company of other writers or on a book panel. But there is nothing more boring than someone telling me what he plans to write when that person hasn't produced a word. It sounds like this to me: Blah, blah, blah. I'm sounding cranky now, right? Oh, well.

Fourth, when I'm not writing, I'm thinking about plots, characters, dialogue, the perfect description of a book I'm going to review. This often happens during my long commute from the West San Fernando Valley to my office in downtown. In other words, much of my writing happens before I actually sit before the computer.

Finally, there is an element of writing that I have trouble explaining but I'll give it a try. Words want to come out of me and take shape in the form of a story, poem, essay, or book review. I am incapable of subduing these words. If I don't get them out of my head and onto paper, I will explode. I'm lucky that some folks have wanted to publish my words, sometimes even paying me. But I suspect that I'd write no matter what. That's why God created blogs. Now go forth and write. You have no excuses!

Valley Chicano Writer Explores the Holocaust

Jewish Journal (2010)

Virtually every student of fiction has been admonished: "Write what you know!" This does not mean that every short story or novel should track the author's life in exquisite detail, though certainly some successful writers have taken that road. What it does mean is that fiction can seem more "real" if the writer speaks with authority borne of experience.

Thus, it's not much of a stretch for me to write a scene where my protagonist is an attorney who has to drive in rush hour traffic on the 101 from West Hills to downtown on a Tuesday to his office in the Ronald Reagan State Building on Spring Street in the Old Bank District.

On the other hand, I would have to do a lot of research to create a comparable scene taking place in Miami, Florida since I've never set foot there. It's certainly not impossible and many talented writers do exactly that every day. But if I attempt this, how "real" will my writing feel to a resident of Miami? I promise you, if I fail, a reader from that city will track me down to explain in six different ways what a failure I am as a writer. It will not be pretty.

It's not surprising that I have often drawn upon my life for material and inspiration. Thus, many of my characters are Chicano or Mexican who live in Los Angeles, either near downtown (where I grew up), or in the West Valley (where I now live with my family). I spent my childhood in a working class neighborhood and attended twelve years of Catholic school. After high school, I left L.A. for Stanford University where I majored in English, and then back to my hometown to attend law school at UCLA. By day, I'm a government lawyer. I have drawn upon all of these elements of my life to populate my fiction.

I also fell in love with my law school sweetheart, Sue, in 1981 and started my Jewish journey. The granddaughter of Russian-Jewish immigrants, she introduced me to wonderful books about Judaism which became part of my informal studies toward conversion. We married in 1986 in a Jewish ceremony; two years later I converted. Our son was born in 1990, attended a Jewish day school for eight years, and became a Bar Mitzvah at thirteen. We also suffered through that horrific hot August day ten years ago at the North Valley Jewish Community Center when Buford Furrow entered the campus where our son played in the back field with his friends.

All of these Jewish experiences have ended up in my fiction, not to mention becoming themes for my poetry, essays and book reviews. At first, I hesitated to draw from this part of my life because, as a convert, I have often felt a bit insecure about my Jewish identity. But I eventually got over that. Indeed, my children's book, *Benjamin and the Word / Benjamín y la palabra* (2005), is about a Chicano-Jewish boy who encounters bigotry on the schoolyard. The book received praise from various quarters including Abraham Foxman, National Director of the Anti-Defamation League, who said that it "helps us understand the effect name-calling has on young people and how parents can effectively talk to their children about hate." Foxman's approval of this particular work of fiction meant more to me than any other praise.

But I have another test of authenticity and, so far, so good. My most recent short-story collection, *Anywhere But L.A.* (2009), includes my first attempt at Holocaust fiction. As a convert, how could I even *think* of tackling the subject? Well, I'm stubborn. I'd find a way.

The path I decided to take was as one of an observer. My story is entitled "The Jew of Dos Cuentos" and concerns a Mexican-born writer who squanders, through alcohol and womanizing, a promising literary career in New York during the Kennedy years. After his marriage disintegrates, he moves to a small Mexican town where he carves out a hermit's life translating his books from English into Spanish. One day, a stranger visits stating that he has admired the writer's books for many years. This stranger, who speaks Spanish with a slight accent, makes a request: Would the writer translate his late wife's memoir from Spanish into English? The stranger explains that he has already translated the original German into Spanish, but it was an exhausting effort and he desires the help of the writer to do the next translation. Intrigued, the writer reads the manuscript which, as it turns out, is a Holocaust memoir.

I don't want to give away any more of my story but I will say that its theme is that we can, through literature, make certain that we never forget the evil that was perpetrated by the Nazis and their sympathizers.

I hope that if you read my story, it will feel "authentic" to you. If not, I am willing to read your e-mails explaining how I missed the mark. But please, be gentle.

INTERVIEWS

Rubén Martínez

Rubén Martínez
Los Angeles Review of Books (2012)

I first met Rubén Martínez three years ago on the campus of Cal State Los Angeles, which hosted the Latino Book & Family Festival that year. I moderated a panel called "Latino LA: The City of Angels Through Fiction, Poetry and Journalism" that included Rubén as well as Héctor Tobar, Julio Martínez, Marisela Norte and Gustavo Arellano. A dream panel, without a doubt: lively, hilarious, and often poignant. What I remember most about Rubén was his intense desire to engage and provoke the audience with both humor and detailed exegesis. It was clear that Rubén not only loved the written word, but he embraced his audience with his entire being.

That day, I also watched Rubén openly wrestle with the complexities and contradictions engendered by his mixed cultural identity: someone of this country, but not quite. He is, in fact, a native Angeleno. But Rubén is also the son and grandson of immigrants from Mexico and El Salvador. As an award-winning author, he has written much on the immigrant experience as well as the political penumbra cast by that volatile subject, including *The Other Side: Notes from the New L.A., Mexico City and Beyond* (1992), *Crossing Over: A Mexican Family on the Migrant Trail* (2001), and *The New Americans* (2004). His heart, mind and soul thrive and struggle in the borderlands.

His latest book, *Desert America: Boom and Bust in the New Old West*, published by Metropolitan Books, brings us to the next stage of the Martínez journey for truth and meaning. This book will challenge every idea you may have formed about life and death in our western deserts, and it will make you question whether we, as sentient beings, have the ability to truly belong to any community other than that within which we were born and raised. It is a compelling and daring book, one filled with equal parts confession, history, and politics. Despite a busy travel schedule to promote his latest literary offering, Rubén kindly agreed to an online interview to discuss *Desert America*.

Q: Your new book is quite a balancing act: to use your own words, "it's a book of reportage, memoir and criticism, an interweaving of radically different narratives: high-end art colonies, and deadly migrant trails, the boutique desert and the desert of addiction and poverty." Did you constantly remind yourself that you were writing in three genres so that the book didn't drift too far in one direction or another?

A: The book developed over a very long period of time. I first thought of writing about the desert probably within a year of arriving in Twentynine Palms, around 1998. My original vision was a book about water in the desert. I was obsessed with it. I'd hike to remote springs and seeps, pored over highly detailed technical maps in search of the miracle of water on trickling down rocks or bubbling up from the sand. It was going to be a book about water rights—but not just about the Colorado River and who steals its water. What about the rights of migrants crossing the desert to the water that would save their lives? Initially it was going to be straight reportage. But all along I was also journaling about "cleaning up" in the desert—slowly leaving behind the addictions that had brought me out to the Big Empty in the first place; that's how the memoir starting taking shape.

The criticism component of the book is essentially an argument about the unholy alliance between artistic representation and speculation in Western art colonies like Taos and Santa Fe (and, much more recently, Joshua Tree, where I also lived), which resulted from the fact that everywhere I turned there seemed to be an old art colony or a new one springing up, during the "boom" years before the crash of 2008. I've always wanted to write across genres, have the self meet the other and history in the text.

Once I was aware that I had three elements to work with, I consciously tried to strike a balance among them. My editor Riva Hocherman at Metropolitan had a lot input on this—counseling me to cut back on the memoir especially, advice that I mostly heeded. (Like all writers, I pushed back on a couple of cuts she suggested!) I mention the writer-editor relationship because I feel so lucky to have had a close working relationship—page by page, word by word—with Riva, who is a marvelous old school editor. I hear horror stories of manuscripts going straight to copy edit these days because of downsizing and bottom-line bullshit in the publishing industry.

Q: Your descriptions of nature are striking. Did you have a literary role model as you painted word pictures of Joshua Tree in California's Mojave Desert, rural northern New Mexico, the art colony in Marfa, Texas, and the Tohono O'odham reservation in southern Arizona?

A: There've been innumerable words written trying to describe the desert West, enough canvases painted for everyone in the country to hang one in their living room, untold photographs and films shot. If anything, I was loath to put another book on the shelf in the "Southwest" section of a used bookstore. Libraries are filled with dusty, forgotten tomes trying to capture the peculiar beauty of this place.

During the years that I was researching and writing and burping babies and just plain blocked, I had different ideas about aesthetic models, or anti-models as the case often was. For example, early on I decided that I would write against Cormac McCarthy: I thought his prose was overwrought and that he was politically and philosophically cynical, if not reactionary (in that the dark portraits he paints leave no room for people to imagine a different world). I was also clear that I never wanted the landscape to overshadow the human figures on the land—this was going to be a book about people, not enchanted natural forms.

But those were to an extent quixotic quests, tilting my sword at discursive windmills that are impossible to deny or erase. McCarthy is unavoidable: he's the Faulkner of the borderlands. Although I still stand by my political and philosophical judgment of him, I ultimately came to grudgingly respect the gnarled curmudgeon. I even borrowed what I consider to be a progressive stylistic trick from him: I'm not sure if he was the first one to render Spanish on the page in roman rather than in italics (thus erasing the border between English and Spanish and no longer "othering" the "foreign"), but he's the first writer who showed me they could get that past an editor or stylebook in New York. (There were certainly many long conversations with my publisher about it, but they relented—the practice is just about mainstream today.) Although this is a book about people, I could hardly avoid the landscape; it's the focus of our desire in the West, with people desiring it at cross-purposes: environmentalists, Hispano loggers, undocumented immigrants, real estate speculators, artists, ATV riders, hunters. My bookshelves are filled with writers and artists and musicians trying to capture the desert. Ana Castillo, the author. Calexico, the band. Obscure monographs from the early 20th century, sketchbooks from the mid-19th century, WPA reports, vintage postcards.

Movies, movies, movies! Two of my favorites: John Ford (*The Searchers*) and Paul Thomas Anderson (*There Will be Blood*). The latter is probably the most important single model I had in the final phase of writing. Anderson's film and the Upton Sinclair *Oil!* novel it was based upon tell the story of the desert West as a place of extreme class conflict, capitalism at its most brutal (an apt allusion for the Great Recession). The rendering of landscape in *There Will Be Blood* is very reminiscent of John Ford—the forms are often brooding, frightening. In lesser Westerns, the landscape is triumphalist, one-dimensional, the Ken Burns effect. I wanted my landscapes to evoke both the beauty we desire and the tension between the sublime and the human drama played out on them.

Q: You recount poignant and sometimes rather humorous encounters with people who have lived in the desert all their lives as well as those who are newcomers to desert life. One of my favorites is your meeting with Denise Chávez's cousin, Enrique Madrid, who lives about an hour's drive from Marfa. Enrique, despite ill health, is what you call a "living encyclopedia of border history," particularly with regard to the mistreatment (often at the hands of the government) of people who live on both sides of the border. When asked, "What do you do with your neighbors?" he answered, in a gentle voice: "You talk to them. You love them. You marry them. You become them."

A: Enrique Madrid, historian and activist in the Big Bend region of West Texas, is the moral center of the book, which is an ethical argument about neighbors. Our literal neighbors—the people that live next door to us. And our more symbolic neighbors—America's relationship to Mexico, for example, or the relations among ethnic groups and social classes that share the same space. Enrique's vision is complicated and contradictory. He is bitter about the devastating legacy of American empire building in the Southwestern deserts. He will forever mourn the death of his neighbor, eighteen-year-old Esequiel Hernández, who was out herding his family's goats in Redford, TX (pop. 100) when he was shot by a Marine unit performing reconnaissance for the "war on drugs" in 1997. The tragedy was an early warning that the global militarized prohibition campaign against drugs is an amoral abomination that does nothing to reduce drug supply or demand, but in fact further corrupts both sides of the border.

On the other hand, Enrique can also wax eloquent about an expansive, Whitmanesque (or Bolivar-esque) notion of the Americas, a great project of integration on all levels—economic, political, cultural. Hanging out in his house, which is both museum and library (thousands and thousands of books and memorabilia and even archeological artifacts), I felt like I was on a Borgesian adventure, that I caught a glimpse of the Aleph itself: that point in time and space that is connected to every other point in history, a coruscating vision of oneness.

There were many other people that I connected to in my desert sojourn that offered me glimpses of key historical moments, particular points of view that had heretofore been hidden from me. Many of them are in the book, some of them are not. My original manuscript was nearly 700 pages long, and that was edited down to a little over 400. My editor decided, probably wisely, that I should not try to compete with the voluble William Vollman.

Q: You say in the book that you "came to the desert to clean up and heal, like the consumptives once did, following the deep symbolic lineage of the desert as destination of restorative pilgrimage, a place to soothe the soul and cleanse the body." Do you think that the desert did this for you? Do you believe that living in a big city makes the healing more difficult so that only a place like the desert can offer healing? I ask because, as you describe it, the desert is not free from drug abuse and temptation.

A: I chose the desert to "clean up" for the symbolic reasons and also for practical ones—the rent was cheap back then (we're talking the late nineties, before the wild season of speculation). The spiritual symbolism for me came after the fact, by the way. When I first arrived in the desert I could not have said what I was doing there. All I knew is that I was broke, broken, on drugs, and that one of the last friends I could count on, performance artist Elia Arce, happened to be in the village of Joshua Tree, part of a fledgling art colony (of course they didn't regard themselves that way at all—that only happened later, when the high rollers came into town).

Later on, as I read more and more about the desert, I realized the spiritual context that I'd stumbled into. Of course, it was no accident that I arrived there. The sense of the sacredness of the desert has actually sharpened for me in the last few years—in spite of the fact that much of the book is about addiction, loss and alienation. A lot of that has to do with striking up a friendship with a theologian at Loyola Marymount University, where I teach. Douglas Christie has committed much of his scholarship to the early Christian monastic tradition, which was a literal journey into the desert in fourth-century Egypt as well as a radical spiritual one, an ancient version of "tune in, drop out, turn on." If initially Doug and I were somewhat suspicious of each other (I judged him a crunchy monk, he thought of me as a hothead postcolonial critic), we found we had much in common. We were both bona fide desert rats. We've been teaching a class together at LMU for the last couple of years, combining spiritual and political lenses to look at the place and the people.

As for my own process of getting clean—both a physical and spiritual path—I went from Mexico City, the most populous place on earth, to the Mojave, one of the loneliest places on the planet. As you say, I soon encountered drugs and death in the desert, but that didn't diminish the potent symbolism of pilgrimage; if anything, it emboldened it. For the last several months I've been working with the Movement for Peace with Justice and Dignity, led by Mexican poet Javier Sicilia, whose son was murdered last year in a cartel-related crime. Almost all of Sicilia's poetry was about the spiritual desert—he was a mystical Catholic poet until his son was murdered and he renounced poetry and translated his verses into activism against the insanity of the drug war, a spark of hope in these, the deadliest days.

The desert is often a phantasmagorical place. When the storm passes, it radiates unique beauty.

Q: Did you ever reach a point where you thought you'd never finish writing this book?

A: Oh yes, many. I moved away from the desert, from northern New Mexico to Los Angeles just as I was starting to write, which separated me from my subject. Various life changes occurred, joyous ones like the birth of our twin daughters, Ruby and Lucía. I continued to wrestle some old demons. Luckily, the Lannan Foundation gave me the amazing gift of one month of writing time at its retreat in Marfa. I wrote 300 pages during that time, in spite of toothaches and panic attacks. The hubcaps were coming off, but I made it through. I must say this: a lot is made of the writer's "solitary" life. For me at least, that's bullshit. I write in a constellation of supportive relationships. There's my wife Angela, herself a writer (her *Pastoral Clinic: Addiction and Dispossession Along the Rio Grande* shares some narrative with my own book, since we lived together in northern New Mexico while she was researching her anthropology dissertation), who is the first responder to all my crises of faith, my editor and publisher; my agent (Susan Bergholz, who has watched my back for fifteen years); friends like David Reid in Berkeley willing to read a draft whenever I needed a fresh pair of eyes, and my dog Bear, rest in peace, who walked me every day in the desert to clear my head.

Q: How has your family reacted to your descriptions of your addictions as well as the addictions of some of them? Do you give family members pre-publication veto power?

A: No veto power, but of course I care about what they think of my self-portraits and how I write the family. Every act of writing the other (especially an intimate other) is an act of betrayal in that the representation never captures the subject in all its fullness. My father is always catching me on inaccuracies—or rather, my memory conjuring one thing and his another. I write in the book that he screened *The Searchers* for the first time in Mexico City. Nope, he says, it was here in L.A. But it was much better for the narrative for it to happen in Mexico City! (I am reminded of that classic Joan Didion essay, "On Keeping a Notebook," in which her memoirs evoke challenges from her intimates. "It wasn't like that at all!")

I have always written and performed material that has plenty of confession in it. I'd like to think I'm striking a balance between the American "I" and the Latin American "We." As far as writing about addiction, I am struck by how "American" a trope that is. We do like our addicts, though we can also crucify them if they lie to us (James Frey). I did decide early on that I would write about my addiction with circumspection, didn't want to get into "too much information" territory, because we've heard it all before. I didn't want this to come across like a VH1 rockumentary about an aging rocker who gets clean in middle age and starts yoga and meditation. I must say that I come from a family that is very American—

notwithstanding our immigrant roots—in the sense that my parents have been nothing but supportive of my career and accepting of almost everything that I write about. My mother, who emigrated from El Salvador as a young woman, went back to school when I was in middle school and eventually received a master's degree in psychology and started a private practice in Los Angeles. I think this had a profound impact on the family in allowing a space to speak of our darkness. My father did alcohol rehab and AA. My sister is a counselor in the public schools, and we all lived, of course, in Oprah's America.

Q: In the end, what do you hope readers get from *Desert America*, or is that something you don't worry about?

A: I definitely want it to be read as a parable about a time and a place: the desert West during the boom and bust of the 2000s. It's a book about desert capitalism, or rather the desert that is capitalism, and about that other desert, the one in our souls, where our ethics spring from to give us the possibility of opening our door to the neighbor or the pilgrim.

Carmen Giménez Smith

Carmen Giménez Smith

La Bloga (2009)

Carmen Giménez Smith is an assistant professor of creative writing at New Mexico State University, the publisher of Noemi Press, and the editor-in-chief of *Puerto del Sol*. Her work has most recently appeared in *Mandorla*, *Colorado Review* and *Ploughshares* and is forthcoming in *Jubilat* and *Denver Quarterly*. She is the author of *Bring Down the Little Birds* (2010), and *Glitch* (2009). She recently edited, with Kate Bernheimer, an anthology of contemporary fairy tale adaptations to be published by Penguin Classics in 2010. She lives in Las Cruces, New Mexico with her husband and their two children.

Carmen kindly agreed to juggle yet one more thing and sit down with *La Bloga* to chat about her new poetry collection, *Odalisque in Pieces* (2009).

Q: How did you decide upon the title of your new collection, *Odalisque in Pieces*? Did you consider other titles?

A: I shuffled through many titles before landing on *Odalisque*. For a long time the book was called *Fussy*, which probably had more to do with my personality than it did with the book. It was called *Solve For N* when I sent it to Arizona; the editors there weren't crazy about that one, so I ordered my husband to come up with a title; he plucked the phrase from a poem in the book. It seemed perfect to me: a woman naked, supine, slavish, shattered.... I feel that it's the book's secret symbol, in a way.

Q: You divide the collection into four sections without titles. Did you intend each section to have a theme?

A: I'd like to think that the book has an arc. Each section contains a poem with a sense of mythos about it, and the book tracks a progression into adulthood. Earlier drafts of the book didn't contain section breaks, but a reader felt that the book needed some moments of pause—some "breathing room," I believe she said—so the section breaks were included to provide something like that. I think the breaks serve to dramatize movement through the book, and also to help ensure that certain significant poems in the book's project wouldn't get lost in the melee of a sectionless collection. To be honest, I'm pretty order-illiterate when it comes to my own work. I've been lucky to have friends who will step in and say, "This is how you should order this book." It may be that poem order literacy is a qualification for a poet's friendship.

Q: One of my favorite poems in your collection is "Tree Tree Tree," which begins: "There's a game we play: / Repeating a word until it ceases to mean...." These lines are both thrilling and horrifying, at least for a writer. Do you ever get lost in words? Do their meanings sometime become obscured the more you dwell with them?

A: I am enthralled by syntax, by the sinews of the sentence. Often my absorption in the line leads to language becoming pure sound for me, something like murmur, but of course the printed word itself and at least the shadow of its meaning always remain. I love Wittgenstein's take on this stuff, the way he seems so utterly perplexed by it, which I think is the correct attitude to take when it comes to thinking about the relationship between the look of the word on the page and the sound of the word in your head or your ear. There's a line somewhere in the Investigations: "Remember that the look of a word is familiar to us in the same kind of way as its sound." I suppose "Tree Tree Tree" speaks to this look–sound problematic in some way.

My first language was Spanish. Writing in a language other than that with which I grew up, with which I learned to think and feel, has surely had some bearing on my relationship to writing. I love finding words and sounds from other languages buried in English; I prefer to imagine discrete languages as continuous, like adjoining rooms connected by a common door—sound. When I revise a poem, I'm thinking primarily about sound, syllables as phonemic puzzle pieces. I wrote "Tree Tree Tree" in graduate school; I think it was exhibitive of my coming to this awareness of new sonic possibilities in my writing.

Q: Do you have a favorite poem in this collection?

A: I have specific, special feelings for each of the poems. The poem "Finding the Lark" took me years and years to write, so I certainly have very strong feelings for that one: something like half ardor, half arduousness. I would write a draft with a truncated ending, and my good friend, one of my best readers, the poet Mark Wunderlich, would hand it back to me and say, "No." When I started writing the poem, I didn't have the chops to sustain the drama, the narrative. I have often seen the necessary course of a poem early on, but have failed to come up with the stamina, I guess, to follow it through all the way to the end. But this is something I'm failing better at all the time.

If I had to choose one poem that's just my out-and-out favorite, I would probably pick "Idea In a Ruinous State," the book's final poem. I'm nuts about Wallace Stevens; early drafts of the poem contained a refrain that included his name. Mark said, "No." I went back to the drawing board. I remember an interim draft that was significantly more expansive. Eventually, I stripped it down into something like a litany, which turned out to be the solution to that particular poem.

As you can tell, my fondness for my own poems concerns the process by which they came to be. Revising and reshaping and reconceiving a poem: that is why I love to write poetry.

Q: Who are some of your favorite poets and how have they influenced your poetry?

A: Well, like I said, Stevens is pretty much the cat's pajamas for me. When I was in graduate school I hated him; I didn't see how earnest his work was until I was older. My favorites list is long and eclectic. My dear friend Rosa Alcalá's work poetry has had a strong influence on my newer work. Her stuff is so nervy and tough; I love it, I love it, I love it. There's Mina Loy, sort of modern dance, and James Wright, wow. Wright's work has been a big force in my life. He's tough too, but also so lyric. I like Neruda's wryness. There's Louise Glück, so terse, the master of compression. Brenda Shaughnessy is so lush, and her beautifully complex syntax. C.D. Wright is great. Juan Felipe Herrera is the sage. Alexander Pope is so funny. Mary Jo Bang has such amazing range. I work with two incredible poets, Connie Voisine and Richard Greenfield; I've learned a great deal from them. They're very different, but both rare talents. Mark Wunderlich is one of the great lyric poets of our time; I've learned so much from him. Some contemporary poets with whom I'm in the early stages of romance are Ariana Reines, Paige Ackerson Kiely, Hoa Nguyen, Peter Ramos, and Dan Machlin.

Q: Do you have a writing routine? How do you juggle writing with teaching and editing?

A: I drop a lot of balls when I juggle.... I have an amazing husband who helps and supports me. I'm blessed with so many generous friends and colleagues.

Once I became a mother, I had to become mercenary with my time. I can't wait around for a poem to strike me, so instead I create goofy scenarios in my mind from which poems might emerge. I have lots of these little multiparous tricks to generate drafts. As soon as my kids are in bed, I write. I also do a lot of composition in my head while I'm doing any number of mundane things, folding laundry, cleaning dishes, etc. I don't necessarily write a poem from memory, but I certainly can imagine a form or an arc, maybe the beginning of a lexicon, then scramble to write it down.

Teaching only fuels my writing. I get so inspired by my students; I often walk away from class jonesing to write, and the work I do as an editor informs my work, as well. I've learned a lot about my own writing from working with authors on their manuscripts. Being an editor and a teacher requires me to quickly and clearly articulate what is at issue in a piece of writing. Surely this has been helpful to my own revision process.

Q: Are you working on another book?

A: I just finished a manuscript of poems called (for now, at least) *Trees Outside the Academy*, as well as another collection called *Happy Trigger*, a book I'm terribly excited about because it's my feminist polemic, the book I've wanted to write for a long time. I've also written a non-fiction book, *Bring Down the Little Birds*, which the University of Arizona Press will release next year. I've been working with Kate Bernheimer—from whom I've learned so much—on an anthology of contemporary writers adapting fairy tales, for publication with Penguin. I've been writing short pieces for a book about money and class called *Squander* and also beginning again to think about a book I've been working on for what feels like eternity, something called *Goodbye Flicker* about a girl who escapes into these fairy tales which her mother has, in the telling, corrupted. I always have to have several projects going on at a time. So many windows open on the computer, crazy stacks of papers around me, books all over the place. It helps me to flit about from thing to thing.

Luis Alberto Urrea

Luis Alberto Urrea
The Elegant Variation (2005)

Luis Alberto Urrea's fiction, non-fiction and poetry have received rave reviews with particular honors heaped upon *The Devil's Highway* (2004), where he brilliantly chronicles the plight of 26 Mexican men who in 2001 crossed the border into an area of the Arizona desert known as the Devil's Highway; only twelve made it safely across. The book received wide acclaim and was a finalist for the 2005 Pulitzer Prize for general non-fiction.

Now Urrea brings us a masterpiece of a novel, *The Hummingbird's Daughter* (2005), which is twenty years in the making. Urrea informs us the story is based on family history and that the young protagonist, Teresita, was his great-aunt. In robust, poetic language, Urrea's novel brings us to the harsh yet thriving landscape of Mexico, circa 1880, where the corrupt government of Porfirio Díaz viciously rules the land. In the midst of brewing revolutionary sentiments, a poor, illiterate and unmarried Yaqui woman (known by her tribe as the "hummingbird"), gives birth to Teresita with the help of the town's curandera named Huila, a cantankerous, powerful and often wise healer who lives in a room in the great hacienda owned by the wealthy, womanizing Don Tomás Urrea. Teresita eventually invades Don Tomás's life through a series of unfortunate events and is subsequently taken under Huila's wing. Huila recognizes Teresita's special abilities as much as she recognizes a family resemblance to Don Tomás who eventually admits to parenthood. The narrative follows the life of Teresita and her family as they confront what Urrea calls the "catastrophe of holiness."

The novel has received the kind of reviews all authors dream of; *The Elegant Variation* published its praises the week *The Hummingbird's Daughter* was released.

Q: One of the things the rave reviews keep on mentioning is the fact that your novel is based on a real person—your aunt. Why did you decide to fictionalize her life rather than attempt outright biography?

A: The simplest answer is you can't footnote a dream. The book has taken many forms over the years of research. But fiction kept asserting itself. I think the magic of fiction is that in many ways it's more true than non-fiction. By that I mean that fiction can take you into truths of feeling and it lends itself better to the kind of trance that allows a reader to smell and taste the world I'm trying to evoke. Also, as a lifelong reader, I can say that I come from a generation where the great achievement was the novel, so, you know, I wanted to try to honor her with an attempt at a masterpiece. You never know if you've gotten there or not, but no guts, no glory.

Q: You mix many elements in *The Hummingbird's Daughter* including both historical facts with what one might call magical realism. Some reviewers imply that you've created a new genre. Have you?

A: I find the magic realism aspects slightly amusing. If only because the things that can be considered "magical" in the text are pretty much the recorded historical facts. During the editing of the book, there were a couple of points where my editor was busy chopping out the real facts and leaving in all the made-up facts so here was a case of truth being stranger than fiction and fiction trying to put mortar between the bricks of astonishment. As far as the "new genre" goes, I refer to Eudora Welty. She said that there is nothing new under the sun, the only thing we have to offer is point of view, so my text, which a reporter told me was baroque, is really an attempt to reproduce those fine semi-addled Mexican voices as they spin out tall tales to their children.

Q: This novel was twenty years in the making. To some, this might look like an obsession. How would you describe your two decades worth of research and writing about Teresita?

A: An obsession. Frankly, you could just as easily say I spent 40 years working on it. Here's the genesis of the text: First, I hear insane folk tales in Tijuana. Second, I live in Sinaloa for a couple of extended periods in my youth and hear more crazy stories. Third, I get a job as a bilingual T.A. in a Chicano Studies department and find out to my astonishment that she was an historical figure and I read a text about her which begins something—I don't know yet what it is. Fourth, I meet a curandero who reveres her and recognizes me immediately as one of her relatives. I start to think hmmm...this could be an interesting thing to pursue. Suddenly, in 1982, I go to Boston to teach at Harvard. You wouldn't think Harvard would open the door to the Yaqui spirits but that's where I found William Curry Holden's book, *Teresita*. I was shocked that there was a book about her. When I saw he had notes and a bibliography, I thought it would be fun to track those sources down. I began tracking sources for several years. In 1990, I moved to Boulder, Colorado, and started hanging out with Linda Hogan and Lorna Dee Cervantes. That's where the real writing began. You can say that I did my book studies between 1982 and 1995. In '95, I moved to Tucson to begin my field work and that's where *The Hummingbird's Daughter* came from. Here's what drove me: I was raised believing she was my aunt. She seems to be some sort of cousin when you work out the genealogical tangles. As I went deeper into her story, I went further into the family tree. I realized quickly that she not only represented my blood, but she represented all the indigenous branches of our family. I realized that her story had been short-changed by Mexican historians, not only because she was indigenous, but because she was a woman. When I started working with shamans, I suddenly got a sense of an afterlife where I came to believe she was currently quite active. And honestly, I woke up one morning and I was older than she was when she died. I started to feel a kind of responsibility to her. It was like growing up. She had been my elder and suddenly, she was a young'un and I felt like I should in some way protect her name.

Q: The characters are so well drawn. I feel like I know Teresita, Huila, Don Tomás Urrea and the others. How much of these characters are based on your research and how much came from your imagination?

A: That's a big reason why it's a novel. You know many facts about these characters, you intuit and synthesize other things. Don Tomás, we know from the record, was a lover and a man of reason. We know that he ultimately sacrificed everything for Teresita. Beyond that, Tomás as a character is a synthesis of all my wildest Urrea cousins in Sinaloa. The character of Segundo is entirely invented—there was no Segundo. There were several cowboys who did various chores that Segundo does in the book, but I needed a foil and a focus for all that male energy. But, perhaps the most important character in the book—Huila—offered me a very interesting problem. If you read the documents, Huila clearly transformed Teresita. However, as is the case in many racist societies, the indigenous woman is erased. To historians in Mexico, Huila was known by her Yori name Maria Sonora, and that's it. The record ends. There is no description of her, not a single quote remaining of hers, there is no knowledge of what her teachings or beliefs were. She has vanished. *The Hummingbird's Daughter* is, as much as anything, an archeological dig to get to the ruins of Huila. I started with the word Huila, which means skinny woman. One of my teachers was my cousin Esperanza. She was trained in the medicine ways by her grandmother, a very powerful Mayo medicine woman. Her name was Maclovia Borbon Moroyoqui. Maclovia was cranky, outrageous, semi-obscene and quite holy. Since she shared traditions and tribal affiliations with Huila, when I learned the Way of Maclovia, I discovered the Way of Huila. For example, the man's scrotum Huila carries in her medicine pouch was something Maclovia was rumored to have acquired.

Q: Some readers of a certain mindset might say that the spiritual elements of the novel help make it a wonderful read but it's all just fantasy. Response?

A: Forgive me for being terse, but it is not fantasy.

Q: Terseness forgiven. Without giving away the ending, it seems that a sequel is quite possible. Any plans?

A: Yes. It wasn't my original intent, but I've already signed a contract with Little Brown so I'm stuck.... Her life broke evenly, if not neatly between the Mexican and the American so her American story is full of incident and tumult. The difference being that it's a turn of the century Industrial American tumult. It's tentatively called *The Queen of America*. Hope it doesn't take twenty years to write....

Q: You've created many relationships in the novel but my favorite is the one between Don Tomás and his daughter, Teresita. Don Tomás is so often exasperated by Teresita's bull-headedness and individuality but, at the same time, he's quite proud of her. Is that based on your relationships with your children?

A: It is largely inspired by my parents' relationship to me, quite frankly. My mother was a New Yorker with a bohemian flair, but deeply conservative views. My father was a Mexican military man and cop with a poet's soul. Neither of them approved of my barefoot love-bead wearing long-haired ways. Yet, they secretly thrilled to my idiotic shenanigans. Far from being the athlete and army captain my father wanted, and even farther from being the crew-cut Ivy League lawyer my mother wanted, I was this post-beatnik art kid. Then, even worse, I became a missionary. What are ya gonna do with a kid like that? Being a dad, however, gave me a whole new perspective. After all, this book is older than all my kids. It's older than my marriage. All the stuff about Teresita as a baby and a toddler...well, that's my daughter, Rosario Teresa. I find myself in a curious spiritual loop here: the baby is named after the character and then affects the way the character's life is narrated.

Q: Did your editor at Little, Brown have much to do with the structure of the novel or the development of the characters? What was your working relationship like?

A: Wow, Geoff Shandler is the best editor you could possibly have. I feel like he and I are a throwback to some of the great author/editor teams of the 1930s, '40s and '50s. Shandler can find the heart of what I'm trying to say, and though he can seem savage with the red pencil, he always gets to the core of what I'm trying to uncover. Think of a movie director like Sam Peckinpah. *The Wild Bunch* is one of my five favorite movies of all time. Anyone can see, however, that it is as much a triumph of editing as it is of direction. Both *The Devil's Highway* and *The Hummingbird's Daughter* bear the stamp of Shandler. If he left Little Brown, I would do everything in my power to follow.

Q: Okay, since I live in Los Angeles, I have to ask: who do you see playing Teresita, Don Tomás and Huila in the movie?

A: I couldn't even guess who could play Teresita. Do you have any hints? Jimmy Smits looks a little bit like some of my nephews and he's very tall like Don Tomás. I think among "my people" Javier Bardem is greatly on the wish list and you know, I look at him and I think put some big whiskers on that guy and he is a great Tomás. He has that certain rakish quality. As for Huila, that would be a very, very special and sacred role for anybody to play. In my heart, she's unplayable. But that's not really true since I gave her all the best lines! It's too bad Lily Tomlin isn't Mexican because I think she could convey the wry power of that woman. I'd like to see that.... Somebody in the Chicano community who is connected to the Teresita story in a lot of ways and who could play a very funky Huila is Denise Chávez. But how 'bout this for a wild suggestion: put a gray wig on her and let the goddess Lila Downs play Huila!

Myriam Gurba

Myriam Gurba

La Bloga (2007)

Myriam Gurba is a high school teacher who lives in Long Beach, California, home of Snoop Dogg and the Queen Mary (as she gamely notes). She graduated from U.C. Berkeley, and her writing has appeared in anthologies such as *The Best American Erotica* (2003), *Bottom's Up* (2004), *Secrets and Confidences* (2004), and *Tough Girls* (2001). Gurba's first book is *Dahlia Season* (2007), a collection of short stories and a novella.

Q: In your heartbreaking story, "Cruising," a teenage girl dresses in male clothing to cruise the pier and public restrooms in Long Beach alongside gay men looking for anonymous sex. When she finally hooks up with a young man and the tryst fails, as it must, she runs away and blames herself: "I had spoiled everything. I ruined it by being myself, by being a girl." This guilt for simply being herself is something that runs through many of your stories. Can you speak a bit to the issue of guilt and how it affects the lives of your protagonists?

A: I hadn't thought about the thematic guilt that runs through my stories, but now that you mention it, I see it very clearly. The narrator of "Cruising" is very mysterious to me and while this character is definitely female-bodied, this person ultimately seems transgendered to me. The guilt experienced by the narrator erupts from physical frustration, being trapped by a body that limits and can't fully express its chameleon self. All my characters have physical circumstances that limit them and they somehow feel responsibility for that although they really have no reason to. I think that this guilt, a guilt experienced by people who feel that their bodies are beyond their control, is part of our unique existential quandary. It's something I've definitely struggled with as a person with Tourette's. I've felt like my body's disobedience is a betrayal that I have to fix and assume responsibility for. Guilt is such a physical thing.

Q: The character of Desiree Garcia in the title novella uses a mordant wit to deal with her Tourette's syndrome and O.C.D. This humor is what keeps the story from falling into bathos. How do you decide which characters will be armed with such humor, and who will not?

A: I knew that if I was going to explore morbid and violent obsessions, I'd have to do so with a spoonful of sugar. Humor became that in the case of Desiree. O.C.D. lends itself very easily to comic writing, but Desiree's unique symptoms are pretty horrifying to her, and I didn't want to minimize that by slathering on the laughs. Other O.C.D. and Tourette's memoirs I've read have been really funny, playing up the silliness of sufferer's compulsions, but I had to pay respect to Desiree's nightmare and exercise caution when it came to timing the funny stuff.

Q: Sex scenes are notoriously difficult to write. Indeed, at least one award is given annually to the worst literary sex scene. But your story "Primera Comunión" has one of the most powerful and honest sex scenes I've read in a long time. Did you hesitate doing such a scene? Was it difficult to write?

A: When writing that scene, I really was inspired by bravery and strength, very macho bravery and strength. I didn't set out to write such a raw sex scene. I had a character in mind, an intensely butch Chicana gangsta. When I was barely, like, thirteen, some white girls made fun of me for being a lesbian. Even then, it was apparent that I was a homo. This gangsta prima of mine who staying with us for the summer shushed these gabachas by telling this scary yet awesome story of a female cholo bad ass vato who nobody denied respect to and it inspired me and comforted me. I was thinking of this cholo when I wrote "Primera Comunión," honoring that vato loco. That mysterious g has served as my muse more than once.

Q: Why did you become a writer?

A: I decided that I wanted to write my senior year of high school. I was in love with all things Sylvia Plath and put myself on a strict writing schedule like I read she'd been on. I filled so many notebooks with writing, but then when my O.C.D. got really bad, I stopped writing. This break lasted throughout my first years at Berkeley. Then, on a lark, I took a class on porn. There were all these writing exercises we got assigned which got me writing again. I started to write a lot about sex and got an internship at On Our Backs, a lesbian pornographic magazine. Since I was in this sex rich environment, my stories reflected that. After I left San Francisco for Long Beach, a lot of sex left my stories. I didn't quit writing, though. I just started to write more about myself and explore other themes.

Q: How did you and Manic D Press get together?

A: In a weird way. Kevin Sampsell, the publisher of Portland-based micropress Future Tense, asked me to submit some stories to *Spork*, a literary journal he was editing. He liked what I sent and asked if I had more. I did and sent it to him. Kevin responded that he does a yearly imprint through Manic D Press and that he wanted to publish my work as a collection. I'm pretty darn lucky to have an offer like that fall in my lap.

Q: What is your writing routine like?

A: Pretty hectic these days. I teach high school so I try to get up around 5 a.m. and write till I have to leave for school. Weekends I give myself a longer time.

Q: Do you have any mentors?

A: Kevin, my co-publisher and editor though Future Tense, has really helped guide me through the publication process. He has been such an inspirational doll. Bett Williams is a new bud but she's been very supportive and nurturing of me, too.

Q: What are you reading these days? Any recommendations?

A: Right now, I'm reading Felicia Luna Lemus's novel *Like Son*. I'm also way into Trinie Dalton, author of *Wide Eyed*. She writes these borderline psychedelic pieces with animals and mythic creatures. I'm re-reading Ali Liebegott's *The Beautifully Worthless*, this genre busting ballad sung to a lonesome America. I plan on reading some of Cookie Mueller's stuff, too. She was one of the Dreamlanders, one of John Waters' actresses.

Q: Any advice for beginning writers?

A: Write. Write, write, write. Don't be afraid to write about yourself. Don't think you need the most epic, adventurous life ever to write and that you need to mine your imagination for these crazy yarns. Tell your stories. Tell your everyday stories. There's plenty of fodder there.

Q: What are you writing right now?

A: Right now I'm working on a graphic novel about how living creatures, human and non-communicate love. Interconnected shorts featuring people, rabbits, and other animals are currently being sculpted into this piece.

DanielAlarcón

Daniel Alarcón

The Elegant Variation (2007)

Daniel Alarcón's fiction and non-fiction have appeared in *The New Yorker*, *Harper's*, *Virginia Quarterly Review*, *Salon*, *Eyeshot* and elsewhere, and anthologized in *Best American Non-Required Reading* (2004 and 2005). He is the associate editor of *Etiqueta Negra*, an award-winning monthly magazine based in his native Lima, Peru. A former Fulbright Scholar to Peru and the recipient of a Whiting Award for 2004, he lives in Oakland, California, where he is the Distinguished Visiting Writer at Mills College. His story collection, *War by Candlelight* (2005), was a finalist for the 2006 PEN/Hemingway Foundation Award.

This February will bring the publication of Alarcón's first novel, *Lost City Radio* (2007). Set in an unnamed South American country that has suffered through years of war and government abuses, Alarcón's novel centers on Norma, the host of a popular program on which she reads the names of missing persons and, in the process, gives hope to callers who desperately want to reunite with lost loved ones. Norma has become a celebrity primarily with those outside the city who live in the mountain and jungle villages. Norma herself nurses the hope of finding her husband, Rey, who disappeared ten years earlier perhaps because of his antigovernment activities. One day, a village boy is brought to the radio station to meet Norma. The boy carries a letter that includes a list of lost people that the boy's village would like Norma to read on her program. But he may also prove to be a link to Norma's missing husband.

Lost City Radio is already garnering advance praise including this from *Booklist*: "A debut novel that is a marvel of concision and soulfulness.... Writing rapturously and elegiacally of the wildness of both the jungle and the city, Alarcón reaches to the heart of our persistent if elusive dream of freedom and peace." David Ulin, book editor for the *Los Angeles Times*, calls Alarcón a "face to watch in 2007."

Q: Why did you decide to set your novel in an unnamed South American country? Why not place it specifically in Peru?

A: In writing this novel, I didn't want to feel restricted in any way by the history, geography, or social landscape of Peru. It wasn't my intention to be coy: I'm Peruvian, the general arc of the war as it unfolds in the novel is similar to that of the Peruvian conflict, and everyone will be able to recognize this. Still, the more I've traveled, the more places I've seen and people I've talked to, the more it has become clear to me that the forces shaping the future of a city like Lima are at work in developing countries all over the planet. When I was on tour last, for *War by Candlelight*, I always found myself saying, "If Peru was an invented country, and Lima an invented city, many people would still recognize it," and I guess I sort of followed my own advice. I invented a country, a city, drew upon my experiences in Lima, upon my travels in West Africa, upon texts I read about Chechnya (the incomparable Anna Politkovskaya), or Beirut, or Mumbai. I was influenced and deeply inspired by the work of Joe Sacco as well, whose books on Palestine and Bosnia are truly masterful. The liberty to call on all kinds of sources was freeing: I came across a book called *Memoirs of an Italian Terrorist*, possibly apocryphal, but it rang so true when compared with the interviews I had done in Peru and Bolivia, that I felt confident referencing it in my attempt to create a composite of what that life might have been like. I am a great admirer of Ryszard Kapuściński as well, and his death today has made me very, very sad. It is a tremendous loss for literature, and personally, I wish most of all that I'd had a chance to tell him face to face how much his work has meant to me over the years. This novel probably owes as much to his influence as to any historical or sociological text of about the Peruvian conflict. Of course, I read many of those as well: Carlos Tapia, Gustavo Gorritti, and Carlos Iván Degregori, just to name a few, have been faithful reporters and brilliant analysts of the conditions that gave rise to the war in Peru.

Q: You note at the end of the novel that you began researching in 1999 and, in the process, interviewed many people about their experiences during Peru's war years. Are there certain interviews that stand out as particularly moving or inspiring?

A: I was living in San Juan de Lurigancho, a district of Lima very similar to the place called Tamoé in the novel. I lived near the market, in a small rented room above a bodega, and taught photography in the neighborhood four days a week. Most of my students lived within a few blocks of me. There was a family down the street whose daughter was in my class, and they sort of adopted me, looked after me, and I would often go over there, to get a meal, or to talk politics with my student's father. They were exceedingly kind to me, and they were folks who had been there from the beginning, since the night the neighborhood was founded, when it was just chalk lines on the barren earth, since the land takeover in 1984. They had come from Ayacucho, the province that gave birth to the Shining Path, and also the region of the country most affected by the relentless violence of the 1980s. I remember one night, it came out in conversation that I had studied anthropology in college, which meant, in actuality that I had taken a set of classes concerned at least superficially with the diversity of human responses to the mystery of being alive on the planet now. I found it difficult to explain that the fact that I had studied it did not mean I was an anthropologist, that the American system of education works differently, that my four year degree qualified me for exactly nothing. The information hung there. "So you can help us," the father said, and I didn't know how to respond, and then quite suddenly, he was gone, away in another room, rummaging through papers. A few minutes later, he came back with lists of the people missing from his village, depositions he had taken of witnesses. He said, "What we've needed all these years is an anthropologist, someone to help us. We know where it is. We know what the army did to them...." I tried to explain, but he wouldn't hear it, and I listened as he described a rather routine army action in the sierra during the 1980s, something that could be accurately labeled a massacre, and he asked me to help him take his village's case to the Truth Commission. This was 2002. The people whose names were typed on the papers he showed me had been dead for fifteen years. "We need an anthropologist," he said over and over. Cultural anthropology, forensic anthropology—it was all the same to him. He wanted me to help him dig up a mass grave.

Q: Was the transition from writing short stories to a full-length novel difficult? Which do you prefer?

A: Everything about writing is difficult, but I do prefer the novel. There is more pleasure in it, more seduction, I think, if only because you spend more time with your characters, and get to know them so well. Stories, by their very form, impose a certain discipline on the narrative impulse that is sometimes hard to accept. In any case, each story demands its own form, and one shouldn't really resist that. I began *Lost City Radio* thinking it was story. Then I called it a long story, then a novella, then a short novel, and didn't use the word novel until it was almost done.

Q: What are you working on now? Another novel? Short stories?

A: A little bit of everything. I spent the fall trying to push various projects past page 40, without much success. I'm onto something now, but I'd rather not talk about it just yet. In the long term, I'd like to write more novels, and also do much more journalism. It's a dream of mine to do a sort of *This American Life* produced in Lima. *Esta Vida Peruana* or something like that. I'm beginning the process of trying make this happen. I would start in Lima, I think with people's stories, first person accounts from the wide range of experiences that exist in the city. Nothing like that has ever been done in Peru that I'm aware of. What interests me most of all are narratives: whether they exist in the world as novels, story collections, radio documentaries, posters or websites is really beside the point. The issue is how to tell the stories that move people, the stories that get at how people live today, and have those stories make an impact. Lima is awash in stories, but for reasons of race, class, geography, etc., we learn very little about each other that isn't alarmist, divisive, or designed to breed suspicion. I've envisioned a radio program, or a series of radio programs that could begin to counteract that.

Q: Has becoming a published author altered your view of literature?

A: No, I wouldn't say that. Being published has made me acutely aware of my preposterous good luck. I have also learned, by necessity, something about the business of publishing, the commoditization of literature, as unrelated to art as a swimming pool is to the ocean. I'm not mad at it—it's simply something I've learned to deal with. Swimming pools are not in and of themselves terrible. But of course, literature is still it: the conversations writers have with the authors who first inspired them—this is the only good reason to do this work. When we write stories we're part of a tradition that stretches back to the beginning of history. The only way I know to approach the blank page is with humility before the scale of what has been already achieved, along with a sense of hope, and above all, playfulness.

Q: Any observations about teaching creative writing?

A: I've come to enjoy teaching quite a bit, which isn't something I could've said a year ago. I taught high school in New York, some undergrad at Iowa, and I taught high school age kids again in Lima, but I wasn't really prepared to deal with graduate students. I had no idea how to do it. As with anything, the more you do it, the easier, the more enjoyable it becomes, but it was pretty touch-and-go there for a minute. When I started, I was trying to finish *Lost City Radio*, trying to learn on the fly, and was in way over my head. My sincere apologies go out to those who had the misfortune of being in my classes a year and a half ago. I'm much more comfortable in front of students now.

Salvador Plascencia

Salvador Plascencia
The Elegant Variation (2006)

Last year, *The Elegant Variation* published my review of Salvador Plascencia's debut novel, *The People of Paper* (2005). I called it "a wonderfully strange, hallucinogenic and hypertextual blending of fiction and autobiography." But I was not alone in singing the novel's praises. The *El Paso Times* proclaimed that Plascencia's "fantastic world...is like inhabiting a poem that tantalizes with its brilliant imagery and imaginative leaps." "New and unexpected," said the *Los Angeles Times*. Plascencia's novel landed on several "best books" lists for 2005.

Most reviewers encountered difficulty trying to explain exactly what this novel is about. Plascencia's characters include Merced, a woman made of paper. There's also a mechanic who makes robot tortoises, flower pickers, gang members, monks, Napoleon Bonaparte, a curandero, among others. Plascencia himself makes an appearance and plays a pivotal role in the narrative. As for the plot, Plascencia's world lives by different rules. And the book's layout is unusual with columns of text vying for attention as but one visual motif. No doubt, it will change your view of what a novel can look like.

Q: The layout and visuals of your novel are so different from more traditional novels. How did you develop the "look" and were there any examples of unusual novels that influenced you?

A: I don't really see *The People of Paper* as a deviation from tradition. If anything, I see it as a throwback to the spirit of early books and to the playfulness that existed before industrialized printing presses. If you look at early books they are very varied in their typography and design. It's a shame that technology has actually limited and uniformed our conception of the book instead of expanding the possibilities. But if I have to claim direct literary influences, like Paul Collins once noted, "All odd books can be blamed on Tristram Shandy," and of course there were Vonnegut and Kathy Acker.

Q: Your book readings are also very different from the typical readings. You employ others to read portions of your book and you also start the reading with what can be called a hilarious monologue that employs a mixture of fact and fiction. How did you develop such presentations?

A: I'm actually a horrible reader. Even if I practice I mumble and mispronounce every other word and I get really nervous. I didn't want to torture the nice people that showed up to the readings with my incoherence, so I had to develop some sort of misdirection to get away from the fact that I can't really read in public.

Q: When your novel came out, you made a comment that caused a bit of controversy within the Chicano writing world. In a *Los Angeles Times* interview, you responded to a question regarding your decision to publish with McSweeney's and not a Latino imprint. You answered: "The Latino imprints never called when it was going around. McSweeney's called. But I'm very happy because now the book doesn't get reviewed as a 'Latino imprint' book, but as a book. As a writer, I align myself with aesthetics, not ethnicity. Why is Jonathan Safran Foer not published by a Jewish American press? Should John Edgar Wideman and Toni Morrison be published only by black presses? There is something comforting in the fact that these ethnic collectives exist, but they can also have a ghettoizing effect."

A: Maybe I'm insensitive to the old school Chicanismo, but I don't see anything particularly inciting about what I said. I just don't have the desire to forefront my ethnicity over my writing. Identity politics bore me, especially when its infighting within the group. A lot of it becomes about people sitting around a table arguing about who is more Chicano and who is a sellout. But who are these arbitrators that get to set the standards of what is Latino or not? It's fair game to critique my book on a aesthetic level, or to call it unreadable, but when it gets knocked for not being Chicano enough or for not fulfilling my ethnic obligation to my group and roots it's a retrograde argument that, to be honest, I'm not really interested in, and it's only minority writers that have to put up with this, and that was my whole point.

Q: Who are your literary influences?

A: Obviously Márquez, and then there is: Ralph Ellison, James Baldwin, Kurt Vonnegut, David Markson, Angela Carter, I remember some and forget others depending on the day. Borges, Morrison, George Saunders, Jiri Grusa, Kafka, Winterson....

Q: I listen to jazz when I write (Miles, Monk, Puente, etc.). Did you listen to music when you wrote your novel? If so, did the music influence your fiction?

A: I didn't have a particular sound track. Whatever was on the radio. A lot of KCRW that I piped in all the way from Santa Monica to Syracuse, New York. I would also listen to what my roommate played on his stereo. He has much better taste in music than I will ever have.

Q: What are you working on now? Another novel? Short stories?

A: I think I'm stuck writing novels for better or worse. I'm too scattered to be able to make one of those tight little machines they call short stories. I'm putting words and sentences together that will hopefully be book number two someday, but I don't have a concrete concept or hook for the second novel. But I had no firm conception about *The People of Paper* either until the final months of working on it.

Q: Why did you write a novel instead of memoir?

A: Why would I write a memoir? When I was writing *The People of Paper* I was a twenty-something kid who came from kind and generous parents, I never fought in a war, and I had nothing but the support and love from my friends and family. What business would I have with the memoir? I'm much more interested in the works of the imagination than in my mundane reality.

Q: What has been the reaction of your family members, friends, ex-girlfriends to your writing?

A: They all do a really good job of not telling me, and I try my best to keep all the copies of my book underneath my bed.

Q: Do you teach writing? If so, any observations about teaching?

A: Right now I'm still a student but I'm looking around some classrooms that I might like.

Margo Candela

Margo Candela

La Bloga (2007)

With the publication this month of her debut novel, *Underneath It All* (2006), Margo Candela introduces Jacquelyn "Jacqs" Sanchez, the fictional personal assistant to the wife of a fictional San Francisco mayor. Jacqs has the brains and beauty (not to mention fashion sense) to survive the political and personal high jinks of her boss, a former soap opera star who finds herself struggling in the role of big city mayor's wife. Jacqs suffers the pain of a failed marriage and battles a slightly self-destructive impulse to pursue men who are simply wrong for her, and there's the culture gap between Jacqs and her more traditional parents and friends back home in Los Angeles. The novel moves along at a fast clip with clever dialogue and memorable characters.

Candela, whose parents came from Mexico, grew up in Los Angeles but attended college at San Francisco State University where she majored in journalism. The middle of five children, she eventually moved back to Los Angeles where she now lives with her husband and son.

Q: Your protagonist, Jacqueline Sanchez, is funny, smart and sexy. Is she modeled on any particular people you know? Also, I really liked the family dynamic between Jacqueline and her parents, who are more traditional than she is. Was that difficult to write?

A: I'll admit to noticing mannerisms and quirks from a wide variety of people I know and incorporating them into different characters, but Jacqueline's mostly a made up person. It made it much more enjoyable to figure out what kind of person she would turn out to be since she was her own person, not based on anyone in particular. She's a little frustrating, but that's what makes her interesting. She's not perfect, she makes mistakes but her heart is (usually) in the right place.

As for the dynamics between her and her parents, it wasn't hard at all to write. Her interactions with them and the rest of her family allowed me to explore some of her flaws and strengths. Her parents are set in their ways and don't understand why Jacqueline insists on rocking the boat, but they love her even though they have a not so obvious way of showing it.

Q: When did you decide that you were going to be a novelist?

A: I wasn't sure how to translate wanting to write into an honest job, so I considered doing something useful like becoming a social worker. When I mentioned this to my mother she wondered why I wouldn't do something in the realm of writing since I seemed to enjoy it so much. It hadn't really occurred to me that I should enjoy my eventual job or even aim for something as ambitious as a career. When it came time to transfer out of junior college I signed myself up as a journalism major (since I figured a job with newspaper or magazine combined my love of writing with my need to be employed) and things developed from there.

Q: Did you have any mentors who helped you on your road to becoming a published novelist? What's the best advice offered to you?

A: I went into this whole thing blind. A lot of the time I faked it, pretending to be comfortable with my decision to take such a huge gamble. Other times I really had to stand my ground to pursuing my goal of getting published. I really didn't have anyone to look to for guidance so I kind of made things up as I went along, setting goals and time frames for myself. When people questioned me or made light of what I was doing, I told them it was like I was starting up and trying to run my own business and, eventually, that mindset gave me more confidence in what I was doing and helped me through some rough spots when things weren't working out the way I'd hoped. In the end, this is a business. Everyone from the agent who signs you to the person who ships your book off from the warehouse thinks of it as such and I think writers should, too.

Q: Who are your literary influences?

A: I've always enjoyed reading Anne Tyler. *Celestial Navigations* (Ballantine Books) is my all-time favorite novel. I read a wide variety of fiction and non-fiction but I don't really have anyone who I can point to as a direct influence of my writing.

Q: Did you listen to music when you wrote your novel? If so, did the music influence your fiction? What is your writing process in general?

A: I have a huge collection of Putumayo compilations on my iPod. They find and put together some of the best world music out there. One of my favorite "finds" is Lhasa de Sela and her song "De Cara A La Pared." I played it again and again when I was working on my literary novel.

I turn my computer on first thing in the morning and turn it off when I can't face it anymore. I set word count goals for myself and it's always a good day when I exceed what I was aiming for. Sometimes I'm really into what I'm working on and time flies, other times I'm sitting at my desk with my head in my hands wondering why I can't write. It's always a huge sense of relief when I finish a manuscript, even though I know I still have to revise and polish it.

Q: What are you working on now?

A: Right now I'm in a bit of a holding pattern. My agent has sent out my novel about three sisters from East Los Angeles whose lives take very different paths before they come back together again and we're waiting to hear from editors. I have two proposals in the works to be presented to my editor at Kensington. The first will be my third women's commercial novel about two people who fall in love but never meet. I'm also hoping to write a young adult book about a girl dealing with the ups and downs of planning for her quinceañera.

Q: What has been the reaction of your family members to your writing?

A: They're very proud of me, but for a long while they were waiting for me to come to my senses and get a real job. I write fiction, but it's inspired by life, and I hope that if they read my books they'll realize any events (or characters) that seem familiar are written out of love and respect. My family and friends are a constant source of inspiration. They do funny, sad, and interesting things I can't help but notice, but I would never intentionally embarrass them or reveal anything private since I want to keep being invited over for dinner.

Q: How did you go about finding a publisher? Any interesting stories that you can share?

A: My editor found me. She had insomnia and a search engine lead her to my site. She sent me an e-mail asking for me to submit, and it couldn't have come at a better time. I had just asked my second agent to release me from my contract and was hoping my current agent was still interested in my work. Within 24 hours I'd met my future editor and found my agent. It's all about timing, perseverance, and a healthy dose of luck. Oh, and the writing. A good manuscript doesn't hurt either.

Q: Any plans for a movie version of your novel? Who do you see playing Jacqueline?

A: I'd love to see *Underneath It All* be turned into a movie, and I don't think many writers out there would say they wouldn't. In my case, especially since there are very few roles out there for Latinas, especially commercial roles, which don't either romanticize or make a caricature out of us. It would be great to see the story brought to life by any of the Latina actresses out there, especially Jessica Alba or Eva Mendes. I think Michael Peña, from *Crash* and *World Trade Center*, would make a perfect Noel, Jacqueline's charming but aimless brother. On the other end of the spectrum, I think Heather Graham could be excellent as Mrs. Mayor, who is a calculating but naïve person.

Q: What are your thoughts about the whole "chica lit" phenomenon? Are you offended by the label? Is the label empowering? What advice would you give to an aspiring Latina writer?

A: I hope readers who like chica lit will like *Underneath It All*, but at the same time I was very conscious when writing it, and my subsequent books, that I wasn't specifically writing chica lit. The writers who have fully embraced the label like Mary Castillo, Sophia Quintero, and, of course, Alisa Valdes-Rodriguez, have turned it into something vibrant and a literary movement that has filled a need for readers. If my book can be included in amongst theirs as well as in the ranks with Jennifer Weiner, I'd be honored. My goal has always been to tell the stories of Latinas while aiming for a general audience. It was very important for me to work with an agent and editor who wouldn't try to make me fit a mold but use my unique perspective as a Latina writing about Latinas to its best advantage.

The only piece of advice I could give to an aspiring Latina writer is to treat the whole experience as a business. You have to invest the time, effort, and make sacrifices to get anywhere in life, writing is no different. There are lots of great resources out there for writers, but don't expect anyone to give you a free pass just because you're a woman or a minority. You have to earn it, just like everyone else. Know what you're writing and why you're writing it. A healthy dose of pragmatism doesn't hurt either, but aim high.

Rigoberto González

Rigoberto González

La Bloga (2010)

Rigoberto González is the author of eight books and the editor of *Camino del Sol: Fifteen Years of Latina and Latino Writing* (2010) recently published by the University of Arizona Press. The recipient of Guggenheim and NEA fellowships, winner of the American Book Award, and The Poetry Center Book Award, he writes a Latino book column for the *El Paso Times*. He is contributing editor for *Poets & Writers Magazine*, on the Board of Directors of the National Book Critics Circle, and is Associate Professor of English at Rutgers-Newark, State University of New Jersey.

Q: What role has the *Camino del Sol* series played in Chicano and Latino literature?

A: Whether the University of Arizona Press was aware of this or not, by championing this literary series devoted exclusively to publishing Chicano/Latino authors for the past sixteen years, the press has been keeping a cultural record of Chicano/Latino literature in the new millennium. The extensive and distinguished list of authors in the series is a veritable who's who and this has made it an attractive place for early-career writers to submit quality work. Thankfully, the series has always kept its doors open to new voices, fomenting an incredible community of artists that will sustain a dynamic and energetic list of talent as the press moves into the next decade. The reputation of Camino del Sol titles continues to grow, solidifying its place as one of the most important and visible Chicano/Latino literary series in the nation.

Q: How long did it take you to compile the poems, stories and essays that were eventually chosen for the anthology?

A: I had read or reviewed for the *El Paso Times* most of the titles by the time Patti Hartmann (the acquisitions editor of the University of Arizona Press) approached me about undertaking this project. But I did have to reread most of the titles (close to 50 books) with the help of my graduate assistant Diego Báez. Together, we read, selected, and retyped all of the entries within one year. Few of the authors had any idea this anthology was being put together, and none had any input on the selections. I wanted to create a narrative of sorts, reflecting the political and social changes that were in the air, and as editor I made the choice to strategize independently. But I was guided by the power and beauty of the writing. This was, I felt, the true testament of the series—how the authors' language, voices and ideas remain relevant to the times and environments we live in.

Q: Did you notice a difference between the earlier pieces and the newer ones?

A: Whatever I come up with in terms of an answer is immediately proven false. About the only thing I can come up with is that the series eventually owned up to the inclusive term Latino. From 1994 to 2001, the series published exclusively Chicano writers, but then came the Caribbean writers like Virgil Suárez and the late Rane Arroyo, and more recently the South American writers Braulio Muñoz, Kathleen de Azevedo, and Marjorie Agosín. There's still room for other traditions and nationalities, and it will be exciting to see what will come next.

Q: Though you were already familiar with the Camino del Sol writers and their works, did you have any epiphanies or encounter any surprises as you dug deep into the catalogue?

A: There were very few books or authors I wasn't already familiar with, but I was pleased to have a chance to reread some of the earlier titles by Juan Felipe Herrera, Demetria Martínez, and Luis Alberto Urrea. I first read those books while I was still in college, so I experienced a pang of nostalgia for the days I was just beginning to discover my literary history and lineage. And look at how far we have all come. (On a side note, I just realized that all three of them were attending the National Latino Writers Conference in Albuquerque last month. It's great to see that they're still active and living examples of generous and productive writers.) Maybe we can add that to the importance of Camino del Sol—it has kept our Chicano/Latino role models in print!

Q: What are your hopes for this anthology? What do you want readers to "get" from it?

A: I think readers will be pleasantly surprised to recognize how aesthetically, politically, and culturally diverse Chicano/Latino literature is. There is no "one way" to shape identity or express it, no "one way" to write as a Chicano/Latino writer in terms of language, subject matter or sensibility. That's a strength, accepting and encouraging our artistic differences, because it will help us come together and move forward in solidarity, especially during these hostile times. Chicano/Latino writers are important, and what we have to say matters. Camino del Sol, the series and the anthology, is not simply a venue for art; it is a venue for life—our lives. It's not only a record; it is a future, and if we don't keep our lives and futures vibrant with poetry and story, it will be that much easier to erase us. Let's keep ourselves living and writing.

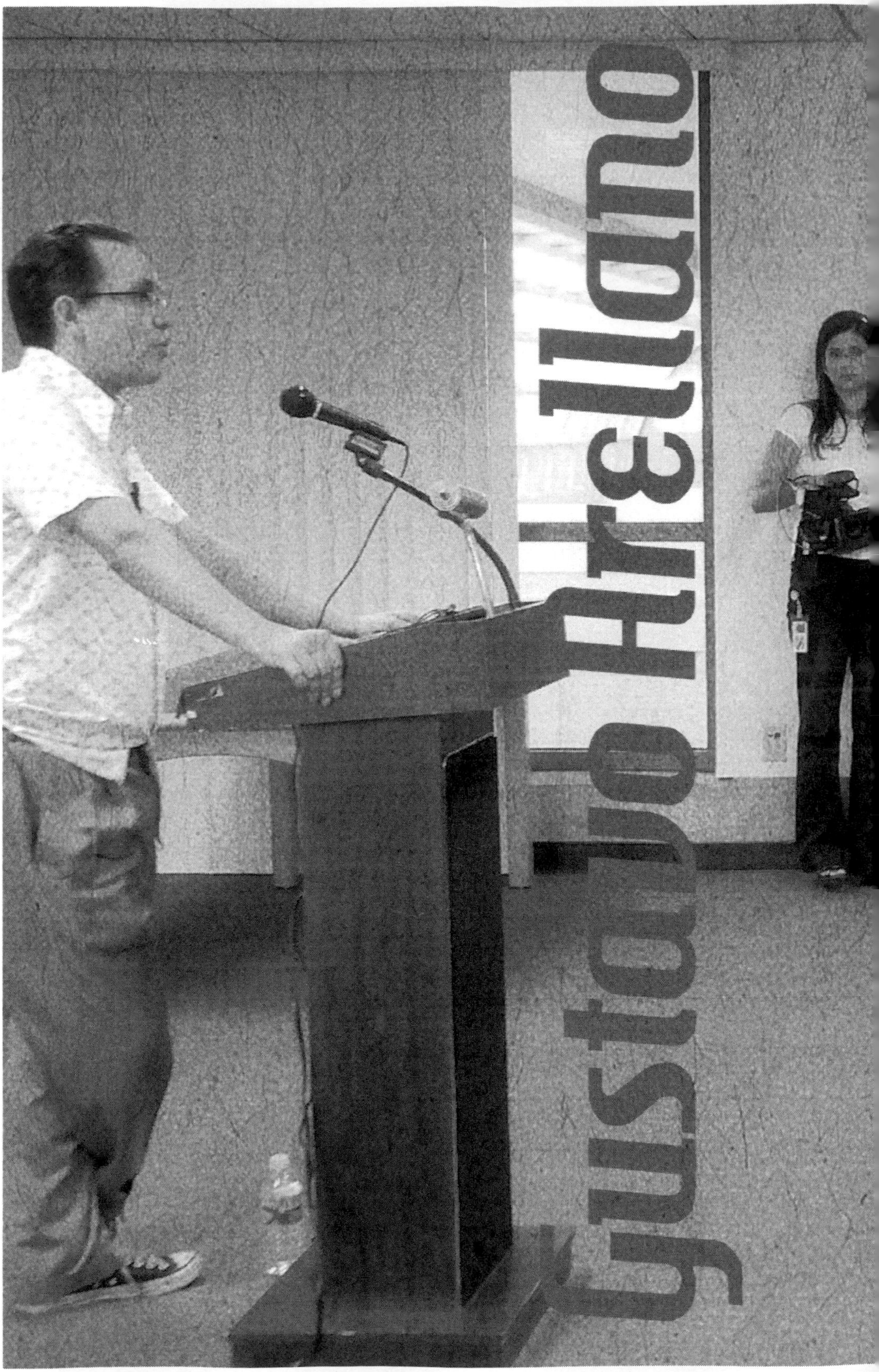
gustavo arellano

Gustavo Arellano

La Bloga (2008)

Gustavo Arellano is a staff writer with the *OC Weekly*, an alternative newspaper in Orange County, California, and a contributing editor to the *Los Angeles Times* Op/Ed pages. He is a familiar presence in Southern California radio as a frequent guest on liberal and conservative talk shows, where he discusses local and national issues. Arellano also writes *¡Ask a Mexican!,* a nationally syndicated column and winner of the 2006 Association of Alternative Weeklies award for Best Column in which he answers any and all questions about America's spiciest and largest minority.

The *¡Ask a Mexican!* column—which will be published in book form by Scribner Press (a division of Simon & Schuster) on Cinco de Mayo 2007—has been the subject of press coverage in the *Los Angeles Times, Detroit Free Press, San Antonio Express-News,* Mexico City's *El Universal* newspaper, *The Today Show, The Situation with Tucker Carlson, Nightline,* the Canadian Broadcasting Corporation's *The Hour, The Tom Leykis Show, Utne,* and *The Colbert Report.*

Arellano's commentaries on Latino culture appear regularly on National Public Radio's *Day to Day* and *Latino USA,* the *Los Angeles Times, The Glenn Beck Show,* and *Pacific News Service.* He was a finalist for the 2005 Maggie Award's Best Public Service Series or Article category for his work on the Catholic Diocese of Orange sex-abuse scandal, a topic for which he was the recipient of the Lilly Scholarship in Religion from the Religion Newswriters Association. Arellano was also a finalist for the 2005 PEN USA Literary Awards for Journalism for his profile on a disabled Latino veteran of the Iraq War. He makes his home in Anaheim.

Q: Did you ever in your wildest dreams imagine that your column would land you a book deal and guest shots on TV and radio?

A: No way. I figured the column would only appeal to those of us in Orange County that find hilarity and a sense of mission in our civic sport of Mexican-bashing, and, really, the column would've remained a naranjero secret if it wasn't for Daniel Hernández, currently of the *LA Weekly* but a member of the *Los Angeles Times* when he did a profile of me last spring. I can boast about the column's appeal all I want, but I'd be just another hard-working, unremarkable Mexican without the *Times*—they made me acceptable and brought forth the book.

Q: Ever get a question you simply couldn't answer?

A: My boast is I can answer any and all questions about Mexicans, and I can—anyone can. The column format allows me to research answers more fully and also grants me the luxury of holding off on more difficult questions—it took me months to find enough material to properly answer why Mexicans use such seemingly ridiculous nicknames (Chuy for Jesús, for instance). But I'll answer a question off the top of my head if I'm on the radio—might not be the best one, but it'll be an answer. That said, why some Mexicans have such an affinity for Thalía will always remain a mystery to me.

Q: Are there any answers you've given that you now regret?

A: Nope. Journalists aren't allowed to regret what they've written—if you do, it's called a retraction, and a good yelling is in store for said scribbler. Though perhaps I shouldn't have uttered the term "butt slut" when I addressed the girls at Smith College last spring....

Q: Were you sent to the principal a lot when you were a kid?

A: Come now! Just because I'm a mocoso now doesn't mean I've always been one. My only sin during los school days was talking too much during class—oh, and one time I threw up in the quad after drinking a gallon of Tampico too fast.

Q: You've gotten flak from some gente basically accusing you of being a trained monkey for the entertainment of Mexican-hating gabachos. Response?

A: People who hate ¡Ask a Mexican! would love to think that only racist gabachos read the column. But those PC pendejos ain't reading me. I probably get as many questions from wabs (the Orange County term for wetback) as I do from gabachos, and a surprisingly large number of queries from Asians and African-Americans. The questions span all topics—rude, intellectual, sexist, ridiculous, perfect. But even if I was a mestizo Bonzo, my trainer (himself a quarter-Mexican) did a bad job—there's a reason why most of my hate mail come from folks who call me an apologist for the Reconquista, and it ain't for my heroic use of pinche.

I want to elaborate on your question a bit further. There's an unfortunate virus in the minds of many educated Chicanos that tells them to call any Latino who doesn't adhere to a blindly leftist, loyalist ideology a vendido—and few Latinos get more grief than journalists. Daniel Hernández received a lot of flak for his coverage of the South Central Farm fiasco even though his reporting was spot-on. Agustín Gurza of the Los Angeles Times—himself a critic of my column—once told me that people called for his job after his stories on the financial troubles of the Ricardo Montalbán Theater. Apparently, they were offended that Agustín dared expose their problems. Those Chicanos/Latinos/mexicanos/whatever-the-hell-they-want-to-call-themselves who whine at the slightest hint of a different public take on a Latino issues come off as the moronic nationalists that the Right portrays all of us as. Criticize us for the wrong facts, not for seeking a truth that sometimes may be ugly.

Q: Which questions do you prefer: those from Mexican-hating gabachos, or those from smart-ass pochos?

A: Both and neither. The best questions are those where I can debunk long-held misconceptions about Mexican culture, from whether George Bush's grandfather really paid a bounty for the skull of Pancho Villa to what part of illegal don't Mexicans understand. That said, it's rather fun to put racists in their place. The smart-ass pochos are merely trying to "catch" me; the Barbara Coes of the world really, truly believe their bigoted drivel and wither away upon facing the light of truth.

Q: Have you met any of your questioners? Were they sober at the time?

A: They were; I wasn't.

Q: Have you thought about franchising your column to cover other ethnic groups?

A: There are already some "Ask a..." columns that cite me as inspiration, namely "Ask a Korean" and "Ask a Cuban-American," while others like Radar Online's "The Ethnicist" and "Ask a Chola" seem like rip-offs to me. Good for them. But contrary to popular belief, ¡Ask a Mexican! isn't my career. Sure, it's garnered me the most fame, but I'm perfectly content telling OC Weekly readers where to eat for the rest of my life in my guise as the paper's food editor.

Q: Are you secretly writing a Mexican version of The Great Gatsby in your spare time?

A: Actually, it's the Zacatecan Grapes of Wrath mixed with Me Talk Pretty One Day and City of Quartz. I'm currently working on a project tentatively titled Orange County: A Memoir. It'll tell the history of Orange County and its significance to America in various regions—political, cultural, etc.—through the saga of my family's four generations in la naranja.

Q: What question do you want to be asked?

A: I get them asked all the time. If I requested a particular question, it would never match the mad, disturbing genius of the Mexican-obsessed American mind.

Aaron Abeyta

Aaron A. Abeyta

La Bloga (2007)

Aaron A. Abeyta is the author of *Colcha* (2001), and *As Orion Falls* (2005). Abeyta received his MFA from Colorado State University and currently teaches at Adams State College. Abeyta is the recipient of the 2001 Colorado Book Award and the 2002 American Book Award. Other awards include a fellowship from the Colorado Council on the Arts and a Grand Prize from the Academy of American Poets.

Abeyta has work published in *An Introduction to Poetry* (10th ed.), *Literature: An Introduction to Fiction, Poetry, & Drama* (8th ed.), *The High Country News*, *The Dry Creek Review*, *S.O.M.O.S.*, *Mountain Gazette*, *Chokecherries*, *Colorado Central Magazine*, and various other journals. He lives in Antonito, Colorado, where he can be close to his roots and family.

Abeyta's latest book is a novel, *Rise, Do Not Be Afraid* (2007), which is a poetically haunting examination of one small town, Santa Rita, as it suffers through the ravages of time and change. Abeyta says that the book "is about the struggle of a community and its people and their attempt to find redemption and meaning while constantly being surrounded by loss. Despite this loss, the characters of the book seek salvation in the only place they know, the interstices of love, faith and nature."

Q: Your previous two books were poetry collections. What prompted you to write a novel?

A: I didn't set out to write a novel. In truth, since most of my poetry has a very narrative thread anyway, I initially sat down to write a poem. My process for poetry, at least at the draft stage, is very let it all out, left to right, full margins and then go back and cut and cut. In this instance, however, I liked the feel of what I had written and it became a chapter in the book. As for making it into a novel and not just a chapter, I had heard about writers that sit down and write every day (that's definitely not me) but I thought, what the heck so I sat down the next day and wrote another chapter. Eventually, I wrote Monday through Thursday with a goal of one chapter per day with revisions and rewrites every night. It was some sort of mad push, but it turned out okay because I was happy with the results.

Q: The novel's structure is not traditional but, rather, it moves freely back and forth in time as it also moves from character to character. Why did you structure your novel in such a way?

A: The easy answer here is also, fortunately, the truth. I wanted the novel to reflect my influences and those influences are very deeply rooted in the oral tradition. Specifically, the ability to hear one story from several different people on several different occasions with the details eventually filling themselves in. In short, I wanted the novel to read as though you were getting the story from multiple perspectives, i.e., from voices past and present.

Q: Is Santa Rita a real place or is it representative of small towns in southern Colorado or elsewhere?

A: Santa Rita is very real, a village in northern New Mexico about one mile from the Colorado Border. My dad used to take me there when I was a kid. Even as a boy I thought the place was beautiful and somehow mythical. You asked earlier what prompted me to write a novel, it was a return trip to Santa Rita, as an adult now, and finding that the road into Santa Rita had been blocked and padlocked, no trespassing signs everywhere. The fact that the place had been bought up by outsiders, and that original inhabitants could no longer go there without a key was, honestly, a big wake-up call for me. In the fate of Santa Rita I began to see parallels with other small towns in New Mexico and southern Colorado, so, to answer your question, Santa Rita is real and representative of small towns.

Q: There are supernatural and biblical elements in your novel. Do you consider it to be in the tradition of "magical realism" or do you reject such categories?

A: I don't reject such categories, but I do believe that there is no such thing as myth if the storyteller is good. As for the tradition of magical realism, I could think of much worse traditions to be associated with. When someone mentions the novel in the same breath as *One Hundred Years of Solitude*, it is a great honor for me and I truly appreciate such connections.

Q: The Bible's influence on your novel is readily apparent especially in your chapter titles. Why did you decide to use the Bible as your touchstone?

A: The Bible, yes, huge influence, but most of the influence came from the Gospel of Luke. I chose Luke for several reasons, but the most evident was that my abuelita used to tell me that Luke's was a gospel of mercy. I didn't know what that meant, but as an adult I began to understand. If you look at corresponding passages from the other gospels you'll see that the translator uses the word "perfect" whereas Luke uses "merciful." Case in point, Dismas the good thief, who died with Christ. Luke is the only one who mentions him in a positive light. In fact, Luke saw to it that Dismas entered into heaven. With Dismas and Luke playing in the back of my mind I chose chapter titles/gospel passages where mercy was evident (at least to me) and used them as the base from which the chapters emerged. I wanted the characters and Santa Rita to be treated mercifully, despite their failings. I guess you could say that all the characters have a bit of Dismas in them, but are redeemed by some form of mercy, rather than perfection. I hope all that made sense. It made sense to me, but sometimes that doesn't count for much.

Q: What was your process in writing this novel? Did you have anyone read early drafts?

A: I think I already answered the first part of this question, but as to the second part...my wife, Michele and my mom were about 24 hours behind me. That is, I would write something on a Monday, and they would read it on Tuesday. Their input was invaluable because it allowed me to verify that I was on the right track with people who knew Santa Rita and some of the people that I based characters on. Once I had their stamp of approval I knew I could continue with the next chapter. I know that having your wife and mom as readers would seem to register about a 0.0 on the objectivity scale, but they were very honest and helped me a lot.

Later, once the entire manuscript was done, I asked a few other people to help. Most of them were very positive, but I did get a few comments about the names of the characters being too difficult. Another reader told me the plot structure was not good. With no offense intended toward those readers, I knew I had done what I set out to do when I received those comments. I didn't want a plot structure that was predictable and I wanted people to see the beauty in the names of the characters. No offense to the Jennifers of the world, but I liked names like Nonnatusia.

Q: Who are your literary influences?

A: Loaded question...here's a very short list in no particular order: Pablo Neruda, Yehuda Amichai, Sandra Cisneros, Sherman Alexie, Lorna Dee Cervantes, César Vallejo, Ernest Hemingway, and Tim O'Brien. There are so many other authors I really look up to that I feel bad not having a list 100 names long, but the ones I did mention all write stuff I identify with on a human and spiritual level, and that's what I wanted for this book.

Q: What do you teach? Does teaching help you as a writer?

A: I teach at Adams State College in Alamosa, Colorado. My two specialty areas are creative writing and Chicano Literature, but I also teach Ethnic & Minority Literature. As for the second part of your question, I think it's the other way around. I think writing helps me as a teacher, mainly because I put a lot of emphasis on being a reader and the connection between reading and writing. Anyway, as writer I feel like I can get a bead on what other writer's are trying to do and therefore convey those things to my students more readily.

Q: What do your friends and family think of your writing?

A: I don't have any friends. Just kidding. My family and friends are very supportive, and both are a great source of material. On one occasion my mom had given me some material, which then turned into a poem for my first book. A while after it was published my aunt came up to me and very seriously asked me, "Where are you getting your information?" I thought that was funny, but it reinforces my earlier point about the same story from different perspectives.

Helen María Viramontes

Helena María Viramontes

La Bloga (2007)

Helena María Viramontes is the author of *The Moths and Other Stories* (1985), the novel *Under the Feet of Jesus* (1995), and the co-editor, with María Herrera-Sobek, of two collections, *Chicana (W)rites: On Word and Film* (1995), and *Chicana Creativity and Criticism: Charting New Frontiers in American Literature* (1988). Her latest novel, *Their Dogs Came with Them,* will be published by Atria Books this week.

Viramontes was born in East Los Angeles into an already large family that always extended itself to relatives and friends who had crossed the border from Mexico to California. After graduating from James A. Garfield High School, she attended Immaculate Heart College, and worked part time at the bookstore and library to help pay for her education. Viramontes took a job as a bottler at the Pabst Blue Ribbon Brewery while taking graduate classes at California State University, Los Angeles. She received first prize for her fiction in the college's *Statement* literary magazine.

A few years later, Viramontes won First Prize in UC-Irvine's Chicano Literary Fiction Competition. She then entered the Graduate Writing program at UCI, but left in 1981 and began to place her stories in small magazines such as *Maize*, and in anthologies, among them the influential *Cuentos: Stories by Latinas*, published in 1983 by Kitchen Table Press.

A community organizer, Viramontes became co-coordinator of the Los Angeles Latino Writers Association and literary editor of *XhistmeArte Magazine* for many years. In the late 1980s, Viramontes helped found the Southern California Latino Writers and Filmmakers. In collaboration with feminist scholar María Herrera Sobek, Viramontes organized three major conferences at UCI resulting in two anthologies. One of her short stories will appear in *Latinos in Lotusland: An Anthology of Contemporary Southern California Literature*, forthcoming from Bilingual Press.

Viramontes' most recent work, *Their Dogs Came with Them,* is a heartrending but hopeful portrait of Chicana lives that are rocked by the turmoil and violence of East Los Angeles during the 1960s. Viramontes kindly agreed to take some time out of her busy schedule to answer a few questions about her new novel, the writing process and other interesting topics.

Q: Why did you set your novel in East Los Angeles circa 1960 to 1970?

A: I set the novel in this decade because of the radical changes happening within the nation and within the community. The discontent with the Vietnam war, the rising power of the disenfranchised and the growing political consciousness planted by Civil Rights, Chicano, and feminist movements all contributed to a chaotic questioning, a disruption of thinking and living. Business was no longer "as usual." Though these were violent and exciting times, there were many who weren't touched by these movements, left out. As the Grandmother Zumaya said of her daughter "whose dreams would be as big as revolutions that did not include you," this is how I felt about several characters. However, Ermila symbolizes for me, a young woman whose feminist consciousness is growing, and who begins to ask "what's wrong with this picture?" She arrives at this question by reading the changes in her community and within herself, and though she doesn't understand, she has a natural intelligence and a moral understanding to begin to realize injustices.

I also thought it interesting to begin the novel with the coming of the freeways. I do remember a time when there weren't any freeways, and then I do remember the neighborhood, whole city blocks abandoned, then chewed up, our neighbors disappeared. It devastated, amputated East L.A. from the rest of the city. The bulldozers resembled the conqueror's ships coming to colonize a second time and I felt a real desire to portray the lives of those who disappeared.

Q: The four female protagonists (Turtle, Ana, Ermila and Tranquilina) appear to struggle with different aspects of human identity. Did you intend these girls/women to represent some kind of archetypal facets of what it meant to be Chicanas in East Los Angeles during the 1960s?

A: As for the four female characters, I'll leave it to the critics as to whether these women are archetypal. However, during the process of writing the novel, I realized that that the characters began to resemble elements. Turtle, fire; Tranquilina, earth; Ermila, wind; Ana, water. But I'm not quite sure how effective or how successful I was. Of course, I didn't plan it that way. Like the mysteries of faith, they slowly began to show themselves as such, and I followed, and yes, these were Chicanas of the sixties. Miraculous, tough caretakers, but survivors of great moral strength. Without them, who gives birth to belief?

Q: The lives of your characters are filled with hardship and violence. Do you see some form of redemption arising from their ordeals?

A: If I didn't want to recognize the redemption of their everyday ordeals, why write about them in the first place? I marvel, truly marvel, at the everyday, ordinary ordeals of human life and I want to give justice to an existence that very few people or readers acknowledge. For example, my brother, who lived with Parkinson's for almost 30 years, is such a hero worthy of attention. Though the illness was to rob him of his independence, my brother Serafin never allowed the humiliation of the disease to remove the dignity by which he chose to live. He painted intense self-portraits, then turned around and painted garden benches, learned calligraphy, nourished beautiful gardens, and painted delicate Chinese symbols. He stumbled and bruised and broke bones, but became a collector of baseball cards, coins, and stamps. He clenched with pain, but was the chronicler, archivist, and organizer of photographs and a recorder of birthdays. He trembled continuously, but molded ceramic bowls, created ceramic flowers, designed wooden angels, sewed buttoned dolls and through it all, his sense of humor remained intact. My brother defied his body constantly by becoming constantly busy. In other words, it simply is amazing to me to see people rise to the potential of their grace in order to survive. I try to honor these unnamed heroes always. I know plenty. We need to acknowledge them, honor them, learn from them in order to live our own lives in a state of grace. To learn hope and the possibility of human will. All this, the whole tortilla, is redemptive.

Q: How does Vietnam play a role in your characters' lives? Do you see any similarity with the current war in Iraq?

A: The short of it is yes. I began the novel, sketching it when the first Iraqi war began, then put down the novel to begin *Under the Feet of Jesus,* and then resumed the novel in 1996 and wrote. But then 9/11 altered our lives forever. The rhetoric of hatred, the chaotic politics mixing with mass hysteria and ultra patriotism was everywhere. A transformation of language began taking place— words were being reduced to essentialist notions, completely violating my sensibility as a writer and as a human being. Flannery O'Connor once said that writers have to read life "in a way that includes the most possibilities—like the medieval commentators on scripture, who found three kinds of meaning in the literal level of the sacred text," and yet we were asked to forgo meaning, bury possibilities, see the world in the most restricted and oppositional way.

I felt I had to get my faith in the written word back ASAP for my sanity's sake. I began to see faith in the written word as a political practice. Because fiction for me is scripture. I had to trust its power to transform chaos into order, aggression into peace, hopelessness into hope. I began to appreciate the capacity of words, their inherent and open meanings, the way I posed to stretch them, invited the reader to participate not as a passive receiver, but contributor of meanings. I began to feel the sacredness of the written word all over again. Though I wrote of the 60s and 70s, now the characters had more agency than ever. They became full characters to me, lovely creatures that no longer haunted me, but lived with me in guarded agreement. I was no longer intimidated by the scope of the novel, and as for the language, I knew, knew, that the magic of flight lay in the language without forgetting once that I am a realist and hope has nothing to do with magic.

Q: You were the recipient of the 2006 Luis Leal Award for Distinction in Chicano/Latino Literature, given annually by the University of California (Santa Barbara), the Santa Barbara Book & Author Festival and Santa Barbara City College. What is the significance of winning this award?

A: The significance for me in winning the 2006 Luis Leal Award was twofold. Firstly, I was greatly honored by UCSB Chicano/Latina faculty, the Santa Barbara Book festival, and Santa Barbara City College committee members that chose me for their annual award. Luis Leal is our national treasure, and I feel greatly inspired by his lifetime of work in Chicano/a studies. Secondly, all the young Chicanas who came to the event brought me to tears. They looked so very proud and I came to understand how truly special this honor was, not just for me, but for all those mujeres in the audience.

Q: Do you believe that writers have any responsibilities to their readers? Do writers-of-color have responsibilities that other writers do not?

A: All serious writers have the responsibility to try and disrupt patterns of thought and behavior that damage the integrity of life. That's why most writers do their best work while living on the fringes of a society. We can have a better view from there. But I think writers of color are no different than both Palestinian writers and Israeli writers who try and capture a community under siege. Because our communities are constantly bombarded with inhumane violence and racism, I think we writers write with greater urgency. I also think we try to provide fictive conditions by which readers will begin a conversation with themselves and the text. The greatest compliment to a writer is if a reader is disturbed enough to begin questioning his/her own beliefs.

Q: How long did it take you to write this novel? What was your writing process like?

A: Not an easy question to answer. I began sketching it in 1991, then dropped it to pay full attention to my novel, *Under the Feet of Jesus*. Then picked up the draft again in 1996. But teaching full time, university obligations, traveling, and mothering kept me incredibly busy. Consequently my writing schedule followed the university seasons: I wrote winter break through early March until my time slowly diminished from weekends to hours to none altogether. Then I had to contain my frustration and sanity until the summer and then write until late September when my time slowly would wither again and on and on it went, year after year.

I do not recommend writing a novel in this way, and it's no wonder that fiction writers in the academy actually become less productive. Writers of novels need to sustain a whole world in their head. We sleep and eat and love with the novel percolating constantly and its continuous dream is determined by continuity of time. When a writer is forced to halt the writing altogether for several months, it becomes time-consuming, frustrating and difficult to resume the threads of the story without first working your head into it once again, be reintroduced into your dream, and precious time is spent on slowly re-submerging yourself back into the story. This seemed to be happening every few months. Writing novels is certainly not for the fainthearted and writing them on a university schedule can be brutally challenging. On writing days, I paced up and down in my office staring at the computer, other times I thought if I moved my computer set up (which I did—from my study for a few years, then into the dining room for a few years— then finally the kitchen—that is until we moved to another house) that these physical movements might help in overcoming my overwhelming insecurities.

Unlike the process of writing *Under the Feet of Jesus*, this novel was so very different, pulling from me rather than filling me, wrenching from me rather than relieving me, and yet, the only thread of hope I had was in trusting my imagination. I knew I had to give in fully in order to let it guide me. The list of characters kept increasing and with this increase, the stories multiplied like freeway interchanges. Having this Eureka moment, I realized that the structure of the novel began to resemble the freeway intersections. I had used something very similar to this in my short story "The Cariboo Café." The intersection structure had always been in the drafts of the *Dogs* novel, but never as strongly until I recognized it. Years later I recognized this same structure in the movie *Amores Perros* and (I admit that it seems easier to pull off these story intersections visually, then to do so using words), and like the freeways upheld by pillars, I realized I had four pillars in four characters of which most other characters orbited around.

On days when the mind and the page went blank, I just kept my fingers close to the keyboard, walking distance close, just in case something would happen. I had to pay close attention. I reminded myself that a novel begins by one word following another. One sentence followed by another. One paragraph followed by another; that discipline, soldier-like discipline was absolutely necessary—as Flannery O'Connor once said, "If there's a great idea somewhere out there, it knows where to find me—between 9-12 at my desk." By working on sentences one at a time, I realized I wouldn't be so intimidated by the scope of the novel. I finally completed the full novel on May 31, 2004.

Q: What books are you currently reading?

A: I am currently reading H.G. Carrillo's brilliant short story "Pornografia," just received the galleys of Manuel Muñoz's new collection of stories *The Faith Healer of Olive Avenue,* and I just finished *Housekeeping* by Marilynne Robinson. Alex Espinoza's *Still Water Saints* is waiting for me. For bedtime reading, I'm 150 pages into Bird and Sherwin's biography of J. Robert Oppenheimer.

Q: Any observations about teaching?

A: What Gabriel García Márquez has taught me when I studied with him at the Sundance Institute: story has no limit.

Manuel Muñoz

Manuel Muñoz

La Bloga (2007)

Manuel Muñoz is the author of a short-story collection, *Zigzagger*, published by Northwestern University Press in 2003. He is the recipient of a Constance Saltonstall Foundation Individual Artist's Grant in Fiction and his work has appeared in many journals, including *Swink*, *Epoch*, *Glimmer Train*, and *Boston Review*, and has aired on National Public Radio's *Selected Shorts*. A native of Dinuba, California, Muñoz graduated from Harvard University and received his M.F.A. in Creative Writing from Cornell University. He now lives in New York City, where he is at work on a novel.

Muñoz's newest book is *The Faith Healer of Olive Avenue: Stories* (2007). *Publishers Weekly* notes of this collection, "Muñoz writes with restraint and without pretension, giving fearless voice to personal tragedies," and *School Library Journal* offers this assessment:

> "With this collection of related stories, Muñoz invites comparison with Gary Soto and Francisco Jiménez. The stories take place in and around Fresno showing the lives of those who stay there, those who leave, and those who return. Most of the main characters are young men, some recently out of high school, who are confronting their futures, and their loves. Although these stories deal with grief and loss, they are neither maudlin nor exuberantly uplifting, but quiet and memorable, the characters taking up residence in readers' minds."

Q: The ten connected stories in your new collection arise from the unforgiving heat of the Central Valley in California where, as you note, people struggle to find meaning "among the houses either crumbling down at the foundation or boasting a fresh coat of paint." How would you describe the manner by which the environment shapes your characters' identities and actions?

A: The Valley is special to me—the more I write about it, the more I become dedicated to keeping my fiction set there. It's a place that doesn't appear with much frequency in American fiction, even in Chicano/a letters: I always feel I'm reading about Los Angeles or Tejas. Geographically, the Valley lends itself to the notion of walls, being bordered on all sides, being entrapped. It stands as a physical barrier to movement, and I love its paradox: when I was growing up, Los Angeles was the dream destination. Crazy, no? Wanting to leave a place of such fertility and green for puro concrete? That's all I need sometimes to keep me writing, the endless well of paradox, of metaphor. The Valley does that for me.

Q: Why did you decide to connect your stories rather than write a novel?

A: I began this collection in September 2002, still a while before *Zigzagger* had been accepted for publication. Many small presses had turned *Zigzagger* down, most with weak-kneed reasoning about reader reluctance to Latino fiction, to gay characters, to the short-story form, and so forth. But I knew I had a good book on my hands and an ever-deepening faith in the short story. I kept writing stories, intent on starting a whole new book. To keep myself on task, I started riffing on a mere mention of three triplets on Gold Street in "Loco" from the first book. Three stories right there, I told myself—and that's where the imagination took over, the clarification of this neighborhood and how it functions, a notion of surveillance, how people watch each other. It never occurred to me that it could become a novel or that it should. I was more interested in the special arcs of the individual stories. A novel would've demanded something over all of them at one time, and I would've had to sacrifice each story's individual nuance to accomplish that.

Q: One of the very fine aspects of your stories is your ability to create characters from all walks of life: male and female, middle class and indigent, gay and straight, parents and children. How do you go about shaping characters who are different from you?

A: Again, back to *Zigzagger.* After the ups-and-downs of its road to publication, I began to believe the many editors who told me that our community wouldn't be ready for fiction with so many gay characters as focal points. When the book was published, I waited for the queer lit community to chime in with some reviews—blog, print...algo. But they were very quiet. I rarely saw my book on their shelves, and it was disheartening. Instead, it was the very Chicano/a community that was allegedly unprepared for this content who rose to the occasion. I'm still taken aback by the speed in which *Zigzagger* has landed on college syllabi, how this community has not pigeonholed the book into any kind of category. I feel proud about the fact that the Chicano/a community treats me like a writer—no adjective needed. I go in to college classrooms and get questions about structure, narrative line, character development: there's a tremendous amount of respect underneath those questions, the unspoken assertion that you're a writer first and foremost.

That feeling began to cement itself very much as I progressed with *The Faith Healer of Olive Avenue*: when you have a community that has faith in your ability in a story, you want to take risks. I began to see the tremendous value in looking at my concerns through various lenses, to challenge myself with points of view and to truly treat these characters like real people. I saw myself broaden as a writer by doing so. I thank the Chicano/a community's response to my first book from promoting that growth, for taking the time to read me and ask questions: I wish I could have received it from the queer community, too, pero ni modo.

Q: In the story "The Comeuppance of Lupe Rivera," a young man named Sergio tells us about his glamorous neighbor, Lupe, who has an unending string of handsome suitors cruising by her home or taking her out on dates. Eventually, violence invades Lupe's life. Sergio, rather than blaming her, tries to make sense out of it: "We all make mistakes—bad luck can ruin everything, even for someone beautiful like Lupe." Does this reflect your philosophy or is it merely one character's attempt at understanding what has happened?

A: It's definitely a little of both. Coming from a place mired in poverty and violence, I still try to make sense of why these conditions are so persistent in my community. During my recent visit to the Valley with Helena María Viramontes, we spoke to a longtime friend of hers, originally from East L.A., who is still dumbfounded by the Valley's general condition as a place to live and work. Did we know, she asked us, that Tulare County was the eighth poorest in the entire country? Growing up in a place like this, I always questioned the fairness of it all, even on a spiritual level. I felt like I lived in a place completely ignored by God (which is one reason why I carry very little religious faith). So much hinged on the whims of nature—a cold snap, a hailstorm, a drought—and suddenly people were out of work and hungry. Growing up like that, you start to look for reasons, however farfetched, and begin to readily accept whatever sounds like the best fit. Sergio, in this story, mirrors that impulse in me—that urge to make sense of the world by shaping a story, even if it's a lie, until you think the edges have rubbed away.

I think you'll find this mechanism at work many times in *The Faith Healer of Olive Avenue*: the mother Connie and her silence with another woman who shares in a tragedy in "Lindo y Querido"; the young troublemaker, Chris, trying to come clean and justify his past wrongdoings in "Señor X"; or the lonelyheart Sebastián, still in love with his adolescent crush on the triplet next door (but unsure which one), in "The Good Brother."

Q: One of the most moving and disturbing stories in your collection is "When You Come Into Your Kingdom." In that story, a father struggles with a family tragedy that grows out of his disappointment with his son. Other stories deal with parental disapproval with their children. What is it about this parent-child relationship that intrigues you as a writer?

A: Ay! I find it so intriguing to have readers point out my compulsions. It really didn't occur to me that I was doing this, focused as I was mostly on a story-to-story basis. But you're right.

I suppose I find this relationship so puzzling because of its tremendous incongruities and complications. Take my stepfather, for example: he married my mother when I was four or five—I hardly remember because he was always around. But that should tell you something. Here was a man from Mexico, barely surviving on his own with fieldwork, who took on the shared responsibility of five children who were not his, and he did it! Can you imagine? What is this about: Love? Honor? Compassion? How do I explain my brothers' initial resistance to him in those early years in the face of this sacrifice? Do you see what I mean by the rich texture of possibility, and that's just my real life!

Tambien, I have to say that, as a gay man, the likelihood of ever having children of my own produces an immense longing. It's a measure of privilege for gay men to adopt or to arrange a surrogate. Here again is the power of the imagination, the breaking apart of the myth of what you wish for: parenting, of course, has to be tremendously difficult, and in my personal longings (like heartbreaks), my way out of that sadness is to build a story around my conclusions, to make something out of my concern and my tristeza that has nothing to do with the initial longing and everything to do with story. That's how and why stories—I think—hit us so hard. We recognize in the ones that touch us the very things that keep us up at night.

Q: Now that you have two books under your belt, what kind of advice would you offer beginning writers? Any special words for Latino/a writers?

A: Be patient. I know it's hard to hear, and I was certainly guilty of throwing up my hands in disgust. But we must practice patience. The publishing world isn't ready to give one of us the whole 25-year-old-wunderkind treatment. Keep our predecessors in mind on those days you get fed up: they had more painful rejections and closed doors than we ever will. Keep writing and make sure you send out only your best work. We are under intense scrutiny now in an ever-tightening market for literature: it isn't enough anymore to rise from a reading inspired to "tell our stories." Now we have to exhibit craft, too, to show that we've got the literary tools to throw some chingadazos if we have to. It may be 2007, but there are more people out there who think Latinos are at a literary event to take coats or serve drinks (believe me—it happened at a journal launch party to me last year). Buy books (and not used ones, por favor—I work in publishing and can't tell you how many times I've heard that Latinos don't buy books!), and you must read voraciously. You can spot a writer who doesn't read by the quality of the sentences.

Q: How did you find your agent, Stuart Bernstein?

A: I met Stuart on Helena's urging. I had actually ignored her advice for several months, having already gone with an agent who ended up doing nothing with my work, but she kept insisting that I at least meet with him. Helena knew of Stuart through Susan Bergholz, the mera mera of agents. Like her, Stuart is proving to be a great champion for our writers and a surprisingly savvy reader. I say surprising because I came up believing that agents serve only the function of mediator between writer and publisher. I'm learning that isn't the case at all. A book, in Stuart's eyes, is never over once it's published. He does quite a bit to keep putting books in front of people.

More than anything, I've learned a new respect for the power of my rights as a writer, especially in this age of digital publishing and the desmadre with Google's attempt to overreach on copyright laws. I'm grateful to have someone in my corner who is patient enough to explain what it all means and has the facility to negotiate terms if need be. For all the work we do as writers, we get very little financial gain from it, and we cannot allow ourselves to be seen simply as "content providers." ¡Por favor! You create the work, whether written or spoken or commissioned for an anthology: why should you give it away to someone else?

Q: What are you reading these days? Any books to recommend?

A: So far, it's been a great year for us in Chicano/a and Latino/a fiction. I just finished Alex Espinoza's superb first novel *Still Water Saints* and have others waiting: Daniel Alarcón's *Lost City Radio*, James Cañon's *Tales from the Town of Widows*, Blas Falconer's poetry collection *A Question of Gravity and Light* (because I'm a big poetry reader, you know) and tambien the forthcoming bigshots, Ana Castillo's *The Guardians* and Junot Díaz's *The Brief Wondrous Life of Oscar Wao*. I'm very anxious to begin dialogues with other writers about Helena's *Their Dogs Came with Them*. Move it up to the top of your piles, please! Her novel is a well of innovation, structural composition, and drive—a perfect marriage of story and craft, made deeper, of course, by Helena's commitment to social justice. But I don't have anyone to talk to about it yet, so hurry up already.

Next up for me is William Henry Lewis's short-story collection, *I Got Somebody in Staunton* (ay, what a great title!). I have a great interest in African-American fiction because it serves as a strong guidepost for our literary community. If you haven't already, take a look at their work from the 1970s, anything from Toni Cade Bambara to Gayl Jones to John Edgar Wideman: you'll marvel at the riches, the huge leaps of faith they exhibit in their storytelling. We have much to learn from their community and their output: you need only look at the current crop of superb young African-American poets like Tracy K. Smith and Kevin Young and Terrance Hayes to see what happens when your predecessors lay out good, solid literature before you like breadcrumbs in the forest. You know exactly where to go next.

Other than that, I always recommend John Edgar Wideman's *Philadelphia Fire*, Joanna Scott's *Arrogance*, Mary Gaitskill's *Veronica*, J. M. Coetzee's *Disgrace*, Ian McEwan's *Atonement*, Joan Silber's *Ideas of Heaven*, Joyce Carol Oates's big-bad *Blonde*, and any of Edward P. Jones's work, but my favorite is his stand-out first collection, *Lost in the City*. Stop me already: I could go on and on.

Q: What are you currently working on?

A: I'm currently writing a novel. It's about a young woman who auditions to sing country songs in a Bakersfield cantina circa 1959 and falls in love. Like all aspiring artists in literature, she's ill-fated and doomed. Pobrecita. That's all I'll say for now.

Q: Who are your mentors? Are you acting as a mentor to new writers?

A: I've talked Helena to the high heavens at this point. I've been on tour with her in California since *Faith Healer* was published a few weeks ago, and I'm still in awe at how students approach her with such reverence and respect. There are all sorts of reasons for it, of course, but it's really her warmth, her commitment, the way her voice quivers with passion when she gets that pointed question about why writing matters at all. She's a phenomenal inspiration, and I'm so lucky to be riding her coattails right now. I feel very proud about putting on a good reading while she's watching, because I know it reflects on her as a maestra, the totality of her presence and influence on our literature. I don't think I had any real idea about it until I saw the lines of students coming to her with nothing but thanks, so I've upped my game, believe me.

I don't act as a mentor to other writers, mostly because I don't teach. I have a nine-to-five copyediting/proofreading job in publishing and hardly ever meet students. I gladly read others' work if approached, but I'm never sure if my readings for them are ever helpful. It can very difficult for me to try to balance being a writer outside of the academy frankly. Around this time of year, I become very jealous of my friends who've worked hard for nine months and now have the summer off to concentrate. I know they're tired, but my work is endless, and the mental strain of reading all day, only to face the desk at night, can be daunting.

I've been taken to task for not teaching by a few other writers, and I respect their opinion, but I follow Helena's mantra. There's more than one way, and mentorship doesn't always have to be one-on-one, cara-a-cara. I count Gary Soto as a mentor, even though I've never met him. Why? Because of the encouraging little note he sent me when he published me through the Chicano Chapbook Series.

Because my high-school English teacher, Dawn Swift, handed me his *Black Hair* when I complained that nobody wrote about the Valley. He reached me even before I became committed to becoming a writer. Same for Lorna Dee Cervantes. Helena brought me to read at a Floricanto in Boulder about ten years ago, and Lorna said to me after my reading that I wrote like a poet (!). I can't write poems to save my life, but to have a writer like her toss off a comment like that gave me something, however tiny, to hold onto when I doubted. Mentors inspire you like that. That's why, as Helena tells me, "Keep working, even though you're tired. Keep your job if that is what is allowing you to get the work done." Because in the same way that I became inspired to pick up a pen when I closed those special books, *The Faith Healer of Olive Avenue* might one day do the same for someone else—mentorship by mere example, mentorship by the power of the book itself.

Sam Quiñones

Sam Quiñones
La Bloga (2007)

Journalist Sam Quiñones lived in Mexico for ten years writing freelance for a variety of United States publications. In 1998, he was a recipient of the Alicia Patterson Fellowship. In 2001, he published a highly acclaimed collection of stories about contemporary Mexico, *True Tales from Another Mexico: the Lynch Mob, the Popsicle Kings, Chalino and the Bronx* (2001). Since its release, *True Tales* has been used in more than 150 university classes at 75 universities in 26 states.

His second book of non-fiction stories, *Antonio's Gun and Delfino's Dream: True Tales of Mexican Migration*, was published in 2007, also by the University of New Mexico Press, and has been greeted with rave reviews from NPR, the *San Francisco Chronicle*, the *Los Angeles Times*, and other publications including a review in yesterday's *El Paso Times* by Christine Granados. Quiñones now lives in Los Angeles with his wife and daughter, and is a staff writer for the *Los Angeles Times*.

Q: Through non-fiction, fiction and satire, such writers as Luis Alberto Urrea, Reyna Grande, and Gustavo Arellano have addressed Mexican migration. How does your book add to this dialogue?

A: I suppose my books try to tell the stories of unnoticed people. My favorite stories to do are those where the people I'm interviewing have never met a reporter.

I don't spend much time on the political/policy side of the immigration issue. I'm more interested in finding poignant stories of real people so I shy away from this debate where the people with the megaphones yell at each other.

But I also don't believe I'm an activist. Activists want only one side of the story. I want it all.

Q: Because undocumented immigration is such a hot button topic, have you encountered vitriol or even threats for your reporting?

A: At the University of Arizona one time people got upset because I said, in response to a question, that I felt that Mexican immigrants needed to assimilate faster, that holding onto Mexico and attitudes born in Mexico, while comfortable, hindered their full participation in the country, and threatened to recreate here in the states what they were escaping in Mexico. Other than that, and my run-in with the Mennonites, which I recount in the book, nothing.

Q: How do you gain the trust of your subjects?

A: I do stories through immersion and repeated interviews and returning often. I find it helps to spend time in a place or with a person, then go away for a while. During this time, I write about the story—maybe record vignettes or write chunks of prose that seem certain to be included in the piece. Then I return, now with a fresh perspective and new questions, which are usually more detailed and focused. I do this over and over. This helps people understand that what I'm after is a fuller sense of who they are, and thus lets them trust me more.

Q: Delfino Juárez's story, in particular, is heartbreaking I think because of his relative youth and his almost unflagging desire to improve his life. What did you, personally, take from his story?

A: I saw firsthand what dedication was, what manhood was, how an ordinary human behaved in extraordinary circumstances, and in all of that, too, I saw just a simple kid trying to make his way, with the foibles and weaknesses we all possess.

I also realized what a disaster immigration is for Mexico because it forces people like Delfino to leave. As I say in the book, his absence would be unnoticed in Mexico, as he is uneducated and unpolished. But this is Mexico's grand delusion—that it really doesn't matter that much that these folks leave. After all, they sent back $23 billion last year, according to the government. What could be wrong with that?

But Mexico is bleeding to death at its border. No one—not the political elite, nor the private sector, the media, churches, the country's right or its left—has been able to put pettiness behind it to confront the massive and wrenching changes the country will need to make to become a country that poor people don't feel they have to leave.

Mexico spends a lot of time fretting over territory it lost to the United States 160 years ago. I don't see anyone taking the loss of these people with the same gravity—though they are the greater loss.

Q: I've had a chance to interview Gustavo Arellano, and I asked him about the flak he's received for his ¡Ask a Mexican! column and subsequent book of the same title. He rejected such criticism and responded, in part: "There's an unfortunate virus in the minds of many educated Chicanos that tells them to call any Latino who doesn't adhere to a blindly leftist, loyalist ideology a vendido—and few Latinos get more grief than journalists." How do you view his form of satire and the criticism he's received from other Chicanos?

A: His column is terrific. Those who criticize it don't understand the subtleties he's getting at. I like his irreverence as well. Latinos, in Los Angeles at least, are the majority population. As such, they need to be scrutinized and have their sacred cows gored. That's healthy and necessary.

I was once criticized for publishing a story in the *Los Angeles Times* about an immigrant woman who had three daughters, then triplets and finally quadruplets, so she had ten kids—the same number her parents had in her village in Jalisco that she had to leave. She's recreated Mexico in Los Angeles, and of course is now mired in virtually inescapable poverty, the same kind her parents faced. Her older daughters, born here, spoke English horribly.

That kind of story needs to be told. The media shouldn't shy away from it.

People get sensitive at Gustavo's column because it's the kind of thing that hasn't been written before.

Q: What grade would you give the "mainstream" press on its coverage of Mexican migration?

A: If you're referring to U.S. TV and radio, then I'd say a D or something. They almost never cover it, and when they do it's very thin.

If you're talking about U.S. newspapers, some of them do much better. Still there's a gap, due to lack of Spanish speakers at many papers, that keeps the coverage at some papers pretty superficial. Also, newspapers need to be more bi-national—that is, they need to send their reporters back and forth between the two countries a lot more, the way immigrants go back and forth. Instead, there are turf battles that keep that from happening. That hinders coverage also. Nevertheless, newspapers are where you're going to see good coverage when it happens.

If you're talking about the Mexican media, they do worst of all. Considering the enormity of the issue for the country, you'd expect better. But they don't understand the United States, since most reporters have never been. They don't understand immigrant Mexico, since they're not from those parts of the country, and often don't have relatives in the states, nor do they understand how to tell stories, as the Mexican media is just emerging from the shadow of 71 years of one-party rule, where reporters were trained to focus on snippets of the political melodrama, avoid going deep, and forget all context or history. With regard to immigration, many just turn to parroting what they've heard about the lives of immigrants in the United States. There's no nuance, subtlety or complexity in what they do.

Q: Your frightening encounter with the drug-running Mennonites really came out of left field. As a journalist, what did you learn from that experience?

A: To understand where I am. I'd had a lot of success penetrating worlds that weren't my own in Mexico up to then. But sometimes you can't.

I never really penetrated that world, as much as I tried. In this case, I was so foolish. I took dumb chances, so I learned to think twice.

Also, I learned that I'll avoid that area from now on.

Q: Who do you enjoy reading?

A: A lot of different stuff. Calvin Trillin is the best journalist storyteller I've read. B. Traven's stories are great as well. I just read the biography of this amateur scientist who both helped found the Jet Propulsion Laboratory in Pasadena and was avidly into metaphysics and witchcraft. He accidentally blew himself up. But he was from that generation that was out there winging it, pardon the pun, untrained, unaware of what couldn't be done.

I just read *Merchant of Venice*—though I didn't like it as much as some of his other plays. John Le Carre is great. Alma Guillermoprieto is, too.

I think writers need to read a lot of varied material. If you ever feel that you shouldn't read something or someone because you wouldn't agree with it, then you should probably read it. Doing that helps jostle your world a bit and that's good. When you have lots coming in from all over, your brain is able to make the connections that lead to better insights. That's my experience, anyway. Also, I read short story writers: Anton Chekhov, John Cheever. Eduardo Parras is hip.

Q: What are you working on now?

A: Two things, mainly.

One, I want to set up my website as a place people can tell their own true tales, or that of a relative, friend, or someone they've encountered. I want stories like Chalino Sánchez sang about: stories of valientes, of immigrants, of narcos. One man's story, for example, is of his days as a cook on a marijuana plantation in the late 1980s.

But also I want stories of minor yet poignant things. I have a story of how I saved the life of a pelican that came out of the sea toward me as I walked along the beach in Mazatlán—that kind of thing. I imagine there are a million of them out there. I want to make the stories tight and readable narratives, with a beginning, middle and end, so I'll edit and rewrite the stuff people send me. But the idea is to make the website a place where people can tell their stories.

So many students I've spoken to tell me about a relative with a wild life story. I'm going to be writing to English and creative writing instructors at universities and junior colleges to let their students know about it.... They should keep in mind that I'm looking for stories of a specific event or moment—a shootout in the hills or how they crossed the border—and told like stories, with a beginning, middle and end, and not just recollections....

The second project is a book of stories about immigrants in Los Angeles—immigrants from Korea, India, Cambodia, as well as from Mexico and Latin America. Los Angeles is what the country is becoming, so I'm hoping the stories will have wider appeal than just here in Southern California. These are stories I've done for the *Los Angeles Times*, but I'll be rewriting them. I'm aiming to get it done by December.

Sergio Troncoso

Sergio Troncoso
La Bloga (2011)

Sergio Troncoso, the son of Mexican immigrants, grew up in El Paso, Texas, and now lives in New York City. He graduated from Harvard College and studied international relations and philosophy at Yale University. Troncoso won a Fulbright scholarship to Mexico and was inducted into the Hispanic Scholarship Fund's Alumni Hall of Fame. He writes the blog ChicoLingo.com about writing, politics, and finance.

Troncoso's first book, *The Last Tortilla and Other Stories* (1999), won the Premio Aztlán and the Southwest Book Award. Troncoso's second book, a novel entitled *The Nature of Truth* (2003), tells the story about a Yale research student who discovers that his boss, a renowned professor, hides a Nazi past.

This year has seen the publication of two more books, one of essays, the other a novel. Troncoso describes his book of essays, *Crossing Borders* (2011), as a "collection that bridges the chasm between the poverty of the border and the highest echelons of success in America, with sacrifice, commitment, and honesty."

Troncoso's new novel, *From This Wicked Patch of Dust* (2011), has at its center the Martínez family that struggles to survive on the U.S.-Mexico border. Troncoso uses this one family to explore issues of assimilation, immigration, religion, politics, and war. It is a story written with great skill and compassion, a story too often ignored or, worse yet, stereotyped by contemporary writers. One would not be surprised to see it included on high-school and college reading lists across the country in the very near future. Of this new novel, award-winning and best-selling author, Luis Alberto Urrea, says: "Sergio Troncoso writes with inevitable grace and mounting power. Family, in all its baffling wonder, comes alive on these pages."

Q: How long did you work on *From This Wicked Patch of Dust*? Did your conception of it evolve as you wrote it?

A: I would guess I worked on the novel for about four or five years. I am always working on several projects simultaneously. Typically, a larger project as an overall focus, and smaller projects, like individual essays and short stories, scattered in and around my schedule for the larger project, so it is difficult to say exactly what amount of time it took me to write the novel. But I also rewrote it, mostly eliminating chapters, condensing it, and sharpening the language. Rewrote it again, and again.

Q: Why did you decide to center your novel on one family from El Paso? Did you have a favorite character?

A: Well, it is a novel, as Lyn Miller-Lachmann correctly appreciates, in which the group, this Mexican-American family, is the protagonist. It is not a novel with an individual protagonist, but something quite different. I wanted to understand the dynamics of group formation, how a family becomes a family, and how it also disintegrates over time. I think this is an inherent tragedy in all our lives, that the family we began with will inevitably disassemble and reconstitute itself (in another form, in another family) if we are lucky. Some of the values, good and bad, are transmitted, some are abandoned, and some are changed to mean something very different from their origin in your "childhood family." This cycle repeats itself, and this cycle is the center of our meaning in the world, at least the way I see it.

I also wanted to focus on the Mexican-American family experience, on "becoming American," whatever that may mean. Why? Because I think any country struggles to remain a country as its inhabitants arrive from different cultures, races, economic levels, urban-rural experiences, and with different individual capacities. As Chicanos become part of this country, not only does this country change them, but they also change the country. These can be religious changes, changes of culture, family practices, so, in a way, the novel is an allegory to what is happening in our country, when individuals adopt different religions, different cultures, different politics. Are we still a group? In what way do the bonds of this group remain vital, but tenuous, and in what way do these bonds evaporate? How can we keep "our family" together?

I also wanted to focus on the variety in the Latino experience, a variety that too often is overlooked. There are Latinos who are Muslim; Latinos who are Jewish, or at least have close ties to Jewish culture and religion; there are Latinos who want to retain a culture focused on Catholicism and paternalistic authority. There are Latinos who are primarily individualists, because of their abilities or political outlooks, still "culturally Chicano" but not really wanting or seeking ties to any group. This great variety is often overlooked, and I wanted to write about that type of multifaceted family.

Q: *From This Wicked Patch of Dust* spans almost 40 years. Accordingly, many historical touchstones are explored including the British Invasion, the Challenger space shuttle, the Vietnam War, 9/11, to name a few. How do you think these events shaped your characters and their destiny? Did you need to do research to refresh your memory of such events?

A: I was constantly doing research on what had happened during particular years, as this family, and its members, become American, grow up, and adopt different attitudes, religions, and so on. Time is very important is this novel. It is written in "time fragments" because I believe that is how families experience their history and how time itself simply dissolves and reconstitutes the original "childhood family," so to speak.

The British invasion of the Beatles is about youth and exuberance and hope, and it matters deeply to the young girl Julia in a way that it won't ever matter to her Mexicano parents Pilar and Cuauhtemoc. Music is often that first separator of generations. I have two teenage boys, fourteen and seventeen, and they live and die for their bands, and I scratch my head and say, "What? That's what you like?" But I was the same way with my parents.

The Space Shuttle Challenger tragedy was a time when we as a country became wounded unexpectedly and deeply, when our hope in science and progress and Reagan's optimism was pierced. Was this another marker when we began to question whether "being American" was synonymous with "progress and hope"? Have we entered another, more nebulous era, when perhaps we are moving backwards as much as we are moving forwards?

Finally, 9/11, when our groundwork belief that we are an invulnerable country, an island against a dark and misunderstood world of danger and fanaticism, exploded along with the Twin Towers. I was in New City when it happened, and it has changed how I look at the world, and how I know we are tied to the world, for better and for worse. Each event sears you closer as a family, as a culture, while it also separates and creates new divisions. 9/11 was the beginning of Latino and immigrant xenophobia, but who would have guessed that 19 radicals, mostly from Saudi Arabia, and professing to be Muslim, would inaugurate that kind of xenophobia years later? The meaning of major events takes time to develop, and involves unpredictable turns. If we had been in the middle of a growing economy, would that xenophobia have been so pronounced?

Yes, these events that occur in the chapters are meaningful to what is happening to the sense of unity or disunity that is also occurring in the Martínez family.

Q: Ismael seems to be closest to you in terms of his education (attending Harvard), marrying a Jewish woman, moving to New York, becoming a writer. Why did you decide to make Ismael merely one of several lives explored in your novel?

A: Ismael is part of his family, and not necessarily its best representative. He has abilities and curiosities that propel him beyond his initial experiences on the border, for better and for worse. Yes, I do identify more closely with Ismael, and it is a favorite character about whom I receive many emails and comments from readers. But I wanted to write about the entire Martínez family experience, in part because I value that variety and different "modes of being" in that family. Francisco's (or Panchito's) experience, staying at home in El Paso and being true to his parents, is as important as Ismael's; the former may not be as exciting or as full of official accomplishments, but I think it is valuable.

On the other hand, Ismael is separated because of his brain, because of who he is, because he sees the world differently, whether he wants to or not. His family does not "cause" him to be the way he is; he is mostly like that already. Yet he still belongs to the Martínez group experience, and yet he still finds meaning in that experience by writing about it. His curious brain and ambition, so to speak, separate him from the group, but these very characteristics also bring him back to the group in a new way, through literature.

Q: What do you hope readers "take away" from your novel?

A: I hope readers take away from my novel that the mysteries of the family, how it comes together and how it falls apart and how it is recreated, are deep mysteries that play out in surprising ways. Characters push and pull in different directions. Yet whatever family experience you had, whether it was decent and heartfelt, or awful and abusive, or simply neglectful, you will have the chance to make it new again, you will also be fighting the worst baggage you inherited, you will also have baggage because of the kind of individual you are. The most surprising "families" exist, some who are Muslim, Catholic, and Jewish all at the same time (and other cultural and religious and political varieties), and why they stay as any kind of "family" at all is because collectively, or individually, or both, they have found meaning in being together while they are alive.

Héctor Tobar

Héctor Tobar

La Bloga (2011)

As a weekly columnist for the *Los Angeles Times*, Pulitzer Prize-winning author Héctor Tobar has eloquently and convincingly challenged his readers' assumptions about the diverse people who imbue this vast metropolis with a complex, thriving and, at times, petulant spirit. As a native Angeleno and the son of Guatemalan immigrants, Tobar's columns often highlight the multifaceted Latino experience by painting exquisite portraits of individuals who want nothing more than to earn a living, get an education or raise a family, and, yes, some of his subjects are undocumented immigrants. Such subjects inevitably produce flurries of angry and sometimes ugly e-mails from certain quarters of his readership. Tobar has been doing this long enough not to be surprised by such a response. Undaunted and apparently energized, he continues to bring these Southern California stories to us, something for which we must be grateful in this age of vitriolic blogs, venal politicians and ravenous 24-hour news cycles.

Tobar now brings us a thrilling and vital novel, *The Barbarian Nurseries*, published by Farrar, Straus and Giroux, where he asks us to consider what would happen if an undocumented housekeeper is wrongly (and very publicly) accused of kidnapping the young sons of an apparently affluent Orange County couple.

The novel has already garnered great advance praise. Dagoberto Gilb says that Tobar's protagonist, Araceli Ramirez, "has flesh, brains, dreams, ambition, history, culture, voice: a rich, generous life. A story that was demanded, we can celebrate that it is now here." And Susan Straight calls the novel "astonishing, like a many-layered mural on a long wall in Los Angeles, a tapestry of people and neighborhoods and stories."

Q: In your weekly columns for the *Los Angeles Times*, you often touch on the issue of immigration. Why did you decide to approach the topic in fiction form?

A: I've been writing books, or trying to, for almost twenty years. Way back in the 1990s, I quit my newspaper job (temporarily) to get an M.F.A. in fiction. I wrote *The Barbarian Nurseries*, a story with an immigrant woman at its center, not because I wanted to write about immigration, but because I wanted to write about the California and the United States of my time. Today, in the country and state I live in, immigration is a defining issue. I'm the son of immigrants, and have lived in California off and on since I was born. I can remember a time of great openness toward newcomers (the 1960s and '70s) and have since seen the evolution of a powerful resentment toward immigrants. That arc of California history is what I've lived. It's shaped who I am and how I see the world. I'm a writer and that life experience is the most important thing I have to write about.

Q: Your protagonist, Araceli Ramirez, a live-in housekeeper for Scott Torres and Maureen Thompson, is judgmental, prickly, and does not like children. Why did you take the risk of putting someone like her in the middle of the immigration debate?

A: Araceli is, in many ways, my alter ego. She's an intellectual trapped in the body of a servant. I am the son of guatemaltecos: to a lot of people in California and elsewhere in the U.S., Guatemalan is synonymous with domestic, with laborer. I come from a humble family filled with people who love ideas and words, which is actually pretty common for Latino families, I think, so I imagined a character who would subvert all the stereotypes about Latino immigrants— especially the myth about their passivity and "fatalism." Araceli is like a lot of Latino people I know or have met: curious, ambitious, but kind of stuck. My book is a novel that attempts to reflect this state of being. It's intended to be a work of art that reflects that tension between what people are, their idiosyncrasies and contradictions, and the labels we place on them.

Q: Orange County and the City of Los Angeles are almost characters in your novel. As someone who grew up in Southern California as the son of immigrants, what was foremost in your mind in depicting the region?

A: I think that I'm most concerned with showing the textures of the California landscape, and of the complexities of the social relationships here: the kinds of things that I don't generally see in works of art (books, film) about Southern California. Among other things, I don't think most people know how old Los Angeles really is, how old it feels in its middle, and how much history is layered there. Similarly, I don't think most people realize how many layers of Latino identity exist here: how "being Latino" can mean so many different things. It's sort of annoying the way we're pigeon-holed as this tragic, colorful people, so I made a very conscious attempt to play against expectations of what a "Latino novel" should look like: among other things, I decided that I had every right to inhabit the eyes and voices of non-Latino characters. You're supposed to "write what you know." What I "know" is L.A. and California: a place that's filled with all kinds of different people. I'm really proud that in my book you'll find people with roots in all sorts of places, Latino and half-Latino, black and white, East Asian and Midwestern.

Q: Scott's struggle with his identity as the son of a Mexican father and white mother is an important thread in your narrative. Why did you decide to make one of Araceli's employers half Mexican?

A: Honestly, that sort of happened by accident. I had decided that I was going to tell the story from multiple points of view, and when I first sat down to create Scott, I imagined him doing what I did when I was a kid: cutting the grass at his home in South Whittier. Now, the South Whittier I lived in, during the 1970s, was a pretty racially integrated place, so, from there, it was an easy thing to imagine him as "half white" or "half Mexican," a status he shares with a big share of the Southern California population, I think. After I decided to give him that identity, other interesting things happened. His Mexican-born father entered the book, for instance, and that gave me the opportunity to make a lot of ironic observations about cultural identity in the city.

Q: The immigration debate never seems to wane; indeed, each election cycle it gets inflamed. What do you think your novel will add to the discussion?

A: More than anything, I think the immigration debate moves forward by denying the essential, complicated humanity of the people who come here. We make immigrants out to be either objects of pity or objects of scorn. In fact, there's a great, complex, many-shaded story in almost every immigrant family. If you take an intimate, honest look at those stories, you'll find universal truths about the human condition. With *The Barbarian Nurseries* I've tried to write a book that gives a hint of those larger truths. It's a book that says this story is part of the thread of the U.S. experience, which is why I've cited three great U.S. writers in the book's epigraphs: Don DeLillo, Richard Wright, and Mark Twain. There's a certain madness to U.S. history when it comes to matters of class and race: a perpetual disorder, a violence, an anger, and, yes, also a hopefulness. The modern-day immigrant story is another unpredictable chapter in the American story: to approach that story as a work of art is to embrace the human craziness of it, which is what I've tried to do in my novel. That's why there's a "lynch mob" in my book, and a Fourth of July extravaganza that fizzles out, and jails, and undocumented scholars, and "orphan boys" and Chicana social workers and police officers, and even a Mexican-American blogger with a defiant, ¿Y qué? attitude.

Carlos E. Cortés

Carlos E. Cortés

La Bloga (2012)

Dr. Carlos E. Cortés is Professor Emeritus of History at the University of California, Riverside. Since 1990 he has served on the summer faculty of the Harvard Institutes for Higher Education, since 1995 has served on the faculty of the Summer Institute for Intercultural Communication, and since 1999 has been an adjunct faculty member of the Federal Executive Institute.

His most recent book is his autobiography, *Rose Hill: An Intermarriage before Its Time* (2012), which traces his upbringing in Kansas City, MO, as the son of a Mexican father and Jewish mother. Other books include *The Children Are Watching: How the Media Teach about Diversity* (2000), and *The Making—and Remaking—of a Multiculturalist* (2002) published by Teachers College Press.

Cortés is general editor of the forthcoming *Multicultural America: A Multimedia Encyclopedia* (2012), Scholar-in-Residence with Univision Communications, and Creative/Cultural Advisor for Nickelodeon's Peabody-award-winning children's television series, *Dora the Explorer*, and its sequel, *Go, Diego, Go!,* for which he received the 2009 NAACP Image Award. He also travels the country performing his one-person autobiographical play, *A Conversation with Alana: One Boy's Multicultural Rite of Passage*, while he co-wrote the book and lyrics for the musical, *We Are Not Alone: Tomás Rivera—A Musical Narrative*, which premiered in 2011.

A consultant to many government agencies, school systems, universities, mass media, private businesses, and other organizations, Cortés has lectured widely throughout the United States, Latin America, Europe, Asia, and Australia on the implications of diversity for education, government, private business, and the mass media.

Q: When did you decide to write the story of your parents and their intermarriage?

A: About ten or twelve years ago, at the request of my daughter Alana, I began writing family sketches—mini-bios, recollections, anecdotes, memorable incidents—in the form of letters to her. Later I assembled them in rough chronological form and filled in narrative gaps. Before I realized it, I had written a sprawling, disjointed 600-page combination family history and autobiography.

At first this was just for the family. But as I began to test the waters by reading excerpts to others, the enthusiastic reactions convinced me that I should try turning it into a book.

A theatre director came to one of my readings and, afterward, suggested that I adapt it into a one-man play. I did and the play, *A*

Conversation with Alana: One Boy's Multicultural Rite of Passage, which I now perform all over the country, has become quite popular, particularly at conferences and universities. More than 120 performances to date.

Performing the play and holding post-performance discussions with audiences helped clarify that intermarriage and its impact on me provided the narrative drive of my story. When I went back to the manuscript, I transformed it from a sprawling 600 pages to a tight 225 pages by focusing on that core narrative of ethnic, religious, class, and linguistic crossfire.

Q: As a historian, did you have difficulty with a subject matter that was so close to your heart and where you played a role?

A: I suppose it might be more dramatic if I said that writing about my family was difficult for me. But that's not true. In fact, telling my story was liberating. The story became more meaningful as I performed, wrote, and discussed it with others, including audiences at the play.

My major challenge was the issue of personal privacy. What things should I omit, if including them would cross the line into unduly exposing other people's lives, particularly when it wasn't essential to the narrative?

Q: Why did you name your book, *Rose Hill*, after the place where your parents were buried? Did you have another title in mind before choosing this one?

A: At first I called it *Letters to Alana* because I wrote the sketches as letters to my daughter. But when I began to shape it into a book, this seemed too much like a gimmick.

I ultimately ended up with *Rose Hill* because the cemetery played such a dramatic role in our family's life both as a source of intercultural conflict and as a magnet for reconciliation and redemption. In the play, my mother's burial at Rose Hill is a climax. On top of that, the title gives off an aura of mystery, beautifully represented by the fabulous cover that my publisher came up with.

Q: Were there any big surprises as you researched your parents' history? Anything you wished you hadn't learned?

A: I didn't really "research" my folks' history. Most of it came from my own memory, challenged by observations from friends and other family members. Probably the biggest surprise was when my wife, Laurel, accidentally came across my folks' love letters, which neither my brother nor I knew anything about.

It may sound strange, but I got to know my parents and grandparents better as I wrote and rewrote and performed so I may have learned more from writing than from research per se.

There's really nothing I wished I hadn't learned, although I must admit those love letters brought a touch of sadness, because they revealed my folks' dreams that were never fulfilled.

Q: What was the reaction of your family when you let them know you were writing this book? What has been their reaction with the finished product? Did you receive any strong objections? Any strong lobbying efforts?

A: At first they seemed somewhat dubious that anyone would want to publish a book about our family or that many people would be interested in reading it. There were also privacy concerns and, quite naturally, concerns about how the family might appear in print. But nobody really objected. The only one who has talked to me about the book since its publication is my brother, Gary, and he seemed happy with it. In fact, he broached the idea of writing a sequel, telling the story from *his* perspective.

Q: Your parents seemed bigger than life. Two people with big hearts, big egos, big tempers, and big dreams? These temperaments seemed to make the intermarriage that much more difficult even taking into account the time and place. Agree?

A: You've nailed it. Their natures and personalities clashed in all kinds of ways. The multiple dimensions of their intermarriage—ethnicity, religion, class, language—served to heighten the conflict, and maybe those factors helped shape their personalities. I don't know exactly what they were like *before* they met. But the structure of society back then, particularly the culture of racial and religious bigotry and segregation, was poised against them. Their personalities made a tough situation more combustible.

Q: Your parents had a secret agreement to divide you and your younger brother, Gary, between the two of them so that you were raised more Mexican and Gary was raised more Jewish. This seems like a recipe for disaster. Thoughts?

A: Readers and audiences at the play have widely varying responses to that decision. In fact, during the play, there is often a gasp when I tell about it. Admittedly it was a strange and maybe radical compromise, but I think it may have been their best option for attempting to save their marriage and trying to remove Gary and me from the family battlefield. Both Gary and I respect their intentions.

Q: Do you have any words of advice for parents whose children are about to marry someone from a different religion or culture?

A: Respect difference. Talk honestly about it. Try to understand alternate perspectives. Don't insist that your own beliefs and concerns are the only ones worth considering.

Encourage your children to talk honestly with their spouses-to-be about those differences, including the way they're planning to raise their children, and when their kids come along, grandparents should support the importance of the grandchildren embracing the *totality* of their backgrounds. Don't pressure them to reject part of their heritage. Let them be whole.

Francisco Aragón

Francisco Aragón
La Bloga (2010)

San Francisco native Francisco Aragón is a poet, translator, essayist, and editor who studied Spanish at the University of California at Berkeley and New York University. He earned an M.A. from the University of California at Davis and an M.F.A. from the University of Notre Dame. Aragón is the author of *Puerta del Sol* (2005), which appears in a bilingual edition where he pairs poems originally written in English with their Spanish-language "elaborations." Aragón's multi-genre book, *Glow of Our Sweat* (2010), includes poems, an essay and translations. Widely anthologized, he also edited *The Wind Shifts: New Latino Poetry* (2007). Aragón is the winner of an Academy of American Poets Prize, and has served on the board of directors of the Association of Writers & Writing Programs. He directs Letras Latinas, the literary program of the Institute for Latino Studies at the University of Notre Dame, and had edited for Momotombo Press, which he founded.

Q: *Glow of Our Sweat* is a hybrid of your poetry and prose as well as poetry in translation. Why did you decide to do this? Were there challenges to this form?

A: As I mention in my "author's note," this wasn't the first time I'd explored poetry "in conversation with" prose, so to speak. *In Praise of Cities*, a "momotombito" chapbook in the wake of 9/11 was my first attempt back in 2002. The feedback was positive. My second attempt, which I didn't mention, was my essay, "The Nicaraguan Novel," which appeared in *Crab Orchard Review*, and which included two embedded poems. That effort garnered positive feedback, as well, so this encouragement facilitated this third attempt, *Glow of Our Sweat*. The novelty this time around was the inclusion of translations. But what dictated this wasn't the desire to add a third "genre," if you will. Rather, it was the subject matter that informed the collection, which came about in an unexpected way.

I'd already been in conversation with Ben Furnish about assembling a chapbook-length manuscript for Scapegoat Press. I'd wanted, for some time, to publish another chapbook. But then something happened, which not only altered the nature of the project, but made me think this gesture (with Scapegoat Press) was turning into something more substantial.

A few poet-friends of mine who were part of the first working group of the Poetry Foundation's Harriet Monroe Poetry Institute recounted an anecdote to me—one which unfolded at the first meeting they had. The anecdote so disturbed me that, after a period of reflection, I decided to assemble a collection of poems that, in one way or another, suggested or insinuated gay or homoerotic themes, though understatedly so. These were poems I'd already published in journals but which weren't part of any collection. I later decided that I would also add translations, using the same guiding principal, and, perhaps more significantly, I decided to write some prose. The result was "Flyer, Closet, Poem." I wrote this essay with the intention of including it alongside the poems and translations. I wrote the first draft of it over a two-week period during a residency at the Ragdale Foundation. I also enlisted María Meléndez and Fred Arroyo to serve as "editors"—above all, editors of the essay. The deeper I got into the project—writing the essay, tweaking the poems, ordering the poems—the more it began to feel like more than a chapbook. In other words, the intellectual and emotional energy I found myself investing in this material—poems, translations, essay, even the notes—began to really work on me, or rather, the process I was undergoing in pulling this project together began to weigh on me. That, coupled with the fact that the collection—with front and back matter—was going to be 72 pages allowed me to wrap my mind around the notion that *Glow of Our Sweat* was, simply, my next book (following *Puerta del Sol*). It also helped that I was able to secure permission from Miguel Angel Reyes to use his stunning print, "Glare," as the cover.

The challenges didn't have to do with the fact that I was mixing genres as much as the questions I had to address in doing so. Which translations was I going to include? How was I going to order the poems? What kind of essay, precisely, was I going to write? Would I include the Spanish originals of the translations and if so, how? Working through these questions was both the challenge and the pleasure. In fact, the last thing I did, was add two translations: the Lorca sonnet and a new translation of Francisco X. Alarcón's "The Other Day I Ran Into García Lorca." Finally, I will say that because I had secured the interest and support of Scapegoat Press, who was sympathetic with the nature of the project, I didn't have to expend energy trying to find and persuade a more conventional publisher to take on a project of these characteristics. I was more than happy to be going with a small press.

Q: You talk about the "coming out" process and proclaim louder than ever that you are a gay man even if, in the past, you were a bit more reticent and "covered" your identity depending on the audience and circumstances. Can you explore this a bit more with us?

A: I'm going to try something unusual here as a way to address this question. I'm going to share with your readers an excerpt of "Flyer, Closet, Poem"—one that fleshes out the disturbing anecdote alluded to earlier, followed by a few comments:

Imagine a young man of nineteen. He's an articulate man who loves to read, who reads poetry and aspires to write. One of his favorite writers is an American poet born near the beginning of the 20th century, and who died when he was just over 40. In this he is not unlike the Spanish poet Federico García Lorca, who was born in 1898, and died at 38. Like Lorca our American poet cultivated the sonnet. One commentator has described our American poet's sonnets as "darkly complex." One of these sonnets has snared our young man's imagination. It's a poem he has committed to memory, a poem whose literary allusions he has looked up, trying to better understand it. The young man, early on, admits to himself that he doesn't necessarily know what the sonnet means. But he loves it. Over time, as he considers the circumstances of his own life—he is African American—the poem begins to speak to him more deeply. It feels like an epiphany—that moment when he finds himself fully inhabiting the poem. It isn't anything in particular the sonnet says, but somehow he comes to feel that the author of the poem—also African American—experienced an isolation not unlike his own. Poem and reader become one. One day, the young man finds himself in a circumstance that affords him the opportunity to share this poem, and his relationship with it on camera. It is a popular national initiative that allows people of all ages, backgrounds, levels of education, etc., to recite a favorite poem and talk about it. The young man is selected to have a modest, but polished video produced, in which he shares his passion for this poem. And he does, poignantly so. In some frames, there is stained glass behind him. In another, he is seated in the pew of a church. For it happens that this young man's faith journey has been important to him. In still another frame, he is walking among trees. He shares his story, some parts of it sad—the derogatory remarks he has endured, the epithets, the feelings of isolation (he also mentions that he is gay). But the poem has been a refuge. Naturally, this American poet's heirs have given permission for their ancestor's sonnet to be a part of this national project. It is a well known poem, often anthologized, easy to find on the internet with a simple Google search. For all practical purposes, it is part of the public domain. What we imagine to be a formality—a copy of the video being sent to the esteemed American poet's heirs—turns out to be otherwise. The estate withdraws permission. The finished video cannot become part of the larger project and be disseminated. Apparently, the poet's estate is on firm legal ground. In essence, this African American poet's heirs are conveying to this living, articulate young African American man: We do not approve of who you are, what you are. And we do not want your likeness, your voice, your name...associated with our esteemed ancestor.

For the record, the sonnet in question is Countee Cullen's "Yet Do I Marvel." I made a decision to keep this information out of the essay in the book, but I no longer feel like doing so. I'm grateful to have this forum to get this information out there and I'll leave it at that.

As I say in the essay, this anecdote haunted me. It was the catalyst for the very book, and I'll add this: my gesture of assembling and publishing *Glow of Our Sweat* was my attempt at being in solidarity with this young man. It was also, in my mind, my way of ceasing to be less reticent about who I am. I might also add that it was a response to The White House's utter lackluster leadership, thus far, on advancing the civil rights of gay, lesbian, and transgender citizens in this country. We seem to be on the cusp where LGBT rights are concerned. I've never considered myself a political poet, but this was an instance where the cliché about the personal being political felt true—at least in my case. Don't get me wrong: in the grand scheme of things, a modest collection of poetry is a blip. But I'm sensing that *Glow of Our Sweat* is a prelude of sorts that's going to lead to more prose, non-fiction prose.

Q: Your book is written in memory of John K. Walsh. What was his influence on you? What did he teach you?

A: I've said, both in private and in print, that I consider myself extremely lucky because of the poetry mentors I've had over the years, both in and out of the classroom. *Glow of Our Sweat* was my way of paying tribute to the mentor who, on a personal level, has meant the most to me. "Jack" was my major advisor at U.C. Berkeley. It was a stroke of good fortune that I chose him. The first time I met him, in his office, we somehow got to talking about Federico García Lorca, even though, officially, modern Spanish poetry wasn't his field. But Lorca was one of his passions, and he passed this passion on to me. I wrote a commentary last winter about the Lorca sonnet I included in *Glow of Our Sweat*. It was a piece for *Poetry Daily* in which I talk about Jack.

In short, Jack was an indelible mentor on two fronts: he invited me to join him in translating Lorca's "Sonetos del amor oscuro," and he shared with me anecdotes about living in Spain as a student, preparing me for my own journey to Spain. He and his long-time partner, Billy Thompson, both did. I spent the 1987-88 academic year living and studying in Barcelona. I had to return to Berkeley for a fifth year to complete my degree, but I already knew I wanted to return to Spain. Jack was the person who suggested I look into "N.Y.U. in Spain" as a way to do this—to pursue a Masters in

Spanish. It turned out that N.YU.'s program offered the option of pursuing a project in literary translation in lieu of a more conventional M.A. thesis. This was a gift since my interest in translation was blossoming at the time. Jack was my guide. My fifth year in Berkeley, on the Berkeley campus, was seminal in some ways: I served as co-editor-in-chief of the *Berkeley Poetry Review*, and it was a year of friendship and mentorship with John K. Walsh. "The Northside Café," the penultimate poem in *Puerta del Sol* (Bilingual Press, 2005), is about that, among other things—including saying goodbye to Jack one August day, the day before I flew back to Spain—not knowing for sure but sensing that I would never see him again. He died the following spring.

Michael Luis Medrano

Michael Luis Medrano

La Bloga (2009)

Michael Luis Medrano is the author of *Born in the Cavity of Sunsets* (2009), his first book of poetry. He holds an M.F.A. in creative writing from the University of Minnesota, Twin Cities, and has performed his work at Stanford University, The Loft Literary Arts Center in Minneapolis, and the University of Colorado, Boulder. He served as poetry editor for the literary journal *Flies, Cockroaches, & Poets*, is featured on the spoken word CD, *The Central Chakrah Project* (Metamorfosis Productions), and has taught writing workshops in Fresno and Minneapolis. Once again based in Fresno, Medrano is teaching, and is the host of *Pakatelas*, a literary radio show on KFCF 88.1 FM. Medrano's latest manuscript, *When You Left to Burn at Sea: Prose Poems & Flash Fiction*, is currently looking for a home.

Q: How old were you when you felt comfortable calling yourself a poet?

A: I was 21 years old, a student in the late Andrés Montoya's Chicano Literature class at Fresno City College. He asked if there were any poets in the class. I raised my hand, cautiously, but I knew I was writing poems at that time.

Q: How long was *Born in the Cavity of Sunsets* in the making? Can you describe its road to publication?

A: The poems in this collection were written between the years 2002-2006. The M.F.A. program (University of Minnesota) was a great place to learn how to shape these poems to reflect a particular voice, to learn how to write a book. My thesis advisor, Ray González, was very instrumental in showing me how to put together the book. Upon completion of the program, I started sending the manuscript to various presses: the big, N.Y. presses and some of my favorite small presses like Curbstone, Tupelo, and of course, Bilingual Press. I avoided book contests because I could not afford to pay the entry fee. I figured to just hit the publishing market the old-fashioned way, send copies of the manuscript and hope for the best. Bilingual Press accepted the book at the end of 2007 after a year and a half of sending the beast out. A year later, and the manuscript entered the editorial process. I credit Bilingual Press for suggesting to eliminate the Spanish glossary from the back of the original manuscript. This made for a more cohesive vision, and the overall book design, masterfully conceived by their talented staff.

Q: Many of your poems concern those who have fallen, either from a difficult life or from disease such as cancer. I view these pieces as both a chronicling of personal histories as well as a form of honoring people who have been taken too soon. How do you view these poems?

A: When I wrote those poems you are referring to I felt it was my way of walking with them, going on the journey, their journey, sharing something simple, like a conversation. The trip wasn't always pretty, but it's their journey, nonetheless.

Q: Which poem in your collection are you most proud of? Why?

A: I'd say "Villanelle: for father & son" because it is a poem that literally helped to shift the role of Medrano patriarch, from my grandfather, Jesús Medrano, to my father, Luis Medrano. My grandfather, before his passing, literally told my father to "take his place." It's poem that chronicles, indefinitely, the passing of a generation.

Q: How do you see the role of the poet in society? What is your role?

A: This question reminds me of how poets/writers (myself included) get when they meet their literary heroes. We get giddy in front of them and often feel short-changed when an expected outcome isn't met. For example, in graduate school I was introduced to a very prominent poet (I will save this person the embarrassment and not mention his name), who shook my hand and stated bluntly upon our introductions, "I guess they'll let anybody in M.F.A. programs these days." Obviously, this is an extreme and very rare example, but the point is to not fully expect that the writer you may meet in person isn't exactly the writer he or she is in person. Think of our past poets, our favorites, as teachers and not as gods.

Q: How would you describe the state of Chicano/a literature? How is it different from where we were twenty years ago?

A: Well, I would say the major difference between the previous generation of Chicano/a poets/writers, and I'm speaking of primarily the generation that came out of the initial Floricanto movement of the late 1960s and early 70s (Juan Felipe Herrera, Lorna Dee Cervantes, Ricardo Sánchez, etc.) was that they did not have Chicano/a literary mentors. We did/do. Now, you can open up a book of poems by Tim Hernandez and compare his work with Sandra Cisneros, and the youngsters today can have their "Aha!" moment when they see the connection between *Loose Women* and *Skin Tax* or you can open up my book and note how I borrowed the music and even the structure of a Martín Espada poem and made it my own. We can do this in much of the same way a Jewish-American writer can open up Ginsburg and see his parallels with Whitman or Lorca, or any other of his well-noted influences—in other words, we can now say we are in the conversation, we are in the game.

Q: Do you have a writing routine? Do you show drafts of your poems to other writers or loved ones to get input before finalizing them?

A: I generally write during the mid-morning hours and after teaching class. I usually work on multiple writing projects, such as now; a prose poem collection I'm fine-tuning, and a longer piece of writing that is aspiring to be a novel. I've stopped showing my writing to my family a long time ago, and this proved to be quite a hairy experience when the book came out. Here were poems, based largely on family truths and taboos, and I had no idea how they were going to handle the experience of seeing their name, in print, in such a critical light. When I presented my family their copies of *BITCOS*, I had to be straightforward with them. Ultimately, I was given their blessing, rather, the correct phrase was "it's your prerogative." Today, I give works in progress to fellow poets and long-time friends, Tim Hernandez, Marisol Baca, and my radio co-host, David Campos.

Q: If you were to recommend three books to a beginning poet, which ones would you choose and why?

A: *Letters to a Young Poet* by Rainer Maria Rilke (Stephen Mitchell translation). In its most basic form, the book is a blueprint on "how" to be a poet. But *Letters* is richly poetic, and by the end of the short book (127 pages!) you have decided whether poetry will be your full-time occupation or not.

Kaddish by Allen Ginsburg: this was one of the first books I read when I first experimented with the prose poem. The title poem, specifically, made me weep. *Kaddish* was my bible during the harsh Minnesota winters, and I could see its influence in my funeral poems.

Sadness of Days: New & Selected Poems by Luis Omar Salinas. I remember when Andrés Montoya brought a small stack of pages photocopied from this collection, and passed them out to the class. He was the one poet I clung to during that semester. The rest of the poets were great also, but it was Salinas's love for justice and his love of love, in other words, generosity, that made his verse a little more sacred than the rest.

Susana Chávez-Silverman

Susana Chávez-Silverman
La Bloga (2010)

Susana Chávez-Silverman is a professor of romance languages and literatures at Pomona College in California. She is author of a memoir, *Killer Crónicas* (2004), and co-editor of *Tropicalizations: Transcultural Representations of Latinidad* (1997), and *Reading and Writing the Ambiente: Queer Sexualities in Latino, Latin American, and Spanish Culture* (2000). Her latest book is *Scenes from la Cuenca de Los Angeles y otros Natural Disasters* (2010), her second memoir from the University of Wisconsin Press.

Q: If you were to describe your new book in a few sentences, what would you say?

A: There are many ways I could describe my book but, hoy por hoy, I'm going to go with a term used by Argentine writer and scholar Walter Mignolo: bi-language love. This book, possibly even more than my last one, is strongly about emotional connection: using a language that is in (at least) two places at once. I use Spanish and English together—as well as their in-between!—to connect with memories, with a sense of wonder and yearning, and with a bunch of important people in my life, also, to connect with other spaces, in a geographical and temporal sense. Of course, I wanted to use this language, these musings and adventures (some of them everyday, some of them more unusual), to connect with the reader, too.

Q: This is your second memoir, the first being *Killer Crónicas*. Is it difficult baring your soul? Would it be easier on some level to fictionalize your life?

A: At first, I was hesitant to have my work characterized as memoir, because the genre is extremely popular, but also recently went through a big ol' backlash, around truth-telling. Plus, I myself found the category too closely associated with a kind of excessive soul-baring. Also, formally, my work somewhat resembles the diary, or correspondence, or even prose poetry, according to some readers. In other words, it doesn't "look" like the standard-issue memoir. People often tell me I could "create such fantastic characters," and ask me when I'm going to write a novel. But I'm not sure my voice would feel as authentic (to me) or sound as authentic (to readers) in fiction—never mind the whole bilingual issue! I'm currently beginning to work on a book about my time in South Africa, where I lived during the 1980s, during apartheid.

Initially I envisioned it as a novel, but in the end, although I believe it will be significantly different from my first two books (longer chapters, probably, moving back and forth between the period in South Africa and the present, for example), I'm fairly certain it won't be fiction. That said, I think the notion that everything in a memoir is "the truth" is naïve, impossible. The act of writing—even when grounded in acts of remembering—always implies an art of composition...and compromise: any writer chooses what to put in, and where, and as important, what to leave out. This book is more "soul baring" than *Killer Crónicas*, in a way; it deals with visceral memories and feelings I didn't even have access to—or interest in—when I was working on *Killer Crónicas*, first in Buenos Aires and later, back home in Califas. But in the end, I would say I still play my cards fairly close to the chaleco, certainly more than the stereotypical "tell-all" memoir writer.

Q: Have any other memoirs influenced you as a writer?

A: It's funny. I haven't really focused on reading memoirs, although I am beginning to more lately, since I am often considered a memoirist. I'm a great lover and voracious reader of fiction and of poetry, mainlyand I'm not too sure about "influence." But I've enjoyed reading (and teaching) Cherrie Moraga's *Loving in the War Years*, and Gloria Anzaldúa, of course. Rigoberto González's *Butterfly Boy*. Also, just off the top of my head, I loved Michael Ondaatje's *Running in the Family*, Emily Raboteau's (autobiographical novel) *The Professor's Daughter*, and very recently, novelist Jane Alison's gorgeous, mesmerizing memoir, *The Sisters Antipodes*.

Q: Do you have a favorite section in your new book? If so, why is it your favorite?

A: Hmmmm, ¡no me gusta play favorites! I honestly don't have a "favorite" section, pero I guess I could say that the one that's probably closest to my heart is the "There Was Blood Diptych," which contains the chapters "Unos Cuantos Piquetitos Crónica" and "Momentos Hemorrágicos Crónica." As for the reason? Bueno, let's just say it was the most difficult part of the book for me to write, and.... I'll leave it to your readers to just "lance themselves." Ándale, dive in!

Ilan Stavans

Ilan Stavans

La Bloga (2010)

Ilan Stavans, a native of Mexico City, is the Lewis-Sebring Professor in Latin American and Latino Culture at Amherst College. An award-winning writer and public television host, his books include *Growing Up Latino* (2004), *The Hispanic Condition* (2001), *The Disappearance: A Novella and Stories* (2006), and *Spanglish* (2004). He is the recipient of numerous honors, including an Emmy nomination, a Guggenheim Fellowship, the Latino Literature Prize, the Antonia Pantoja Award, and Chile's Presidential Medal. For many years he was host of the PBS show *La Plaza: Conversations with Ilan Stavans*.

Stavans is also the general editor of the long-awaited *The Norton Anthology of Latino Literature* (2010). The team of editors includes some of our finest scholars of Latino literature: Edna Acosta-Belén (University at Albany, SUNY), Harold Augenbraum (National Book Foundation), María Herrera-Sobek (University of California, Santa Barbara), Rolando Hinojosa (University of Texas, Austin), and Gustavo Pérez-Firmat (Columbia University).

Q: *The Norton Anthology of Latino Literature* was thirteen years in the making and spans five centuries with the work of 201 writers. It seems that before you and your co-editors could even begin this tremendous endeavor, you had to define two terms: "Latino" and "literature."

A: The terms are at the core of the endeavor, which during the in-house production process came to be known as "*NALL*." The preface to the anthology ponders the various appellations of the Latino minority over time, including Spanish-speaking people, Hispanics, and hispanos, and how each of these appellations fits into a particular historical context. Nowadays, newspapers like *The New York Times*, *The Washington Post*, and the *Los Angeles Times* oscillate, within the same article, between Hispanics and Latinos. In *NALL* the editorial team endorsed the name preferred by the community itself, not the one coming from governmental sources. Personally, I'm less interested in why "Latino" is better than in the forces that keep "the name game" generating so much heat. It seems to me that the ambivalence we feel toward how we should be called is a testament to our never-ending search for a collective identity.

As for the term "literature," *NALL* is open-minded. The anthology not only features short stories, poems, plays, essays, and fragments of longer fiction narratives. It also contains cartoons, blogs, letters, lyrics, dichos, folktales, chistes, children's songs, and political treaties, among other items. In other words, the entries cross freely the artificial border between so-called high-brow and pop lit.

Q: How did you and the other editors divide up the work? Were there many controversies over who or what should be included?

A: *NALL* has more than 2,600 pages. The total number of words is 1,403,804. It includes 3,271 footnotes. The content, organized chronologically, is divided into six major sections, the fifth of which is by far the longest: Colonization (1537 1810), Annexations (1811-1898), Acculturation (1899-1945), Upheaval (1946-1979), Into the Mainstream (1980-present), and Popular Dimensions. The last section features historical documents and essays by prominent Latin American writers on Latinos on life in the United States. *NALL* includes two alternate tables of content: the first reflects the sequence of the material from beginning to end; the second agglutinates entries by nation of origin: Mexican-Americans, Puerto Ricans in the mainland, Cuban-Americans, Central and South Americans, Spaniards, etc.

I was lucky to work with a first-rate editorial team of specialists in various fields: Edna Acosta-Belén (SUNY–Albany) was in charge of Puerto Rican literature in the island and the mainland; Harold Augenbraum (National Book Foundation), of nineteenth-century literature and Dominican American literature; María Herrera-Sobek (U.C.–Santa Barbara), of colonial literature; Rolando Hinojosa (U.T.–Austin), of Mexican American literature; and Gustavo Pérez Firmat (Columbia University), of Cuban American literature.

Controversies—there were plenty! They not only ranged from who should be included to how the material ought to be presented, but to what precise wording to use when describing historical figures like Emiliano Zapata, José Martí, and Lolita Lebrón.

I hope *NALL* generates debate. An endeavor of this scope seeks to engage readers in an ongoing national conversation, and all national conversations are about consent and dissent.

Q: Were there authors you wished could be included but weren't?

A: Sure. One particular author, who shall go unmentioned, should have been in—and vice versa. This is inevitable! The manuscript submitted to the publisher, containing almost two million words, needed to be cut. Permissions also marked our choices. Still, *NALL* is as close to my original vision, my utopian vision, as is possible in our imperfect universe. Working with the Norton editorial team was a dream: I run out of words when describing their superb work ethics.

Q: Were there any real surprises for you? Did working on the anthology change any of your beliefs about Latino literature?

A: Surprises galore, Daniel. The project changed me more than I'm able to acknowledge. I hope one day to describe, in honest fashion, the labyrinth that I and the editorial team found ourselves in and our various encounters with the Minotaur.

Q: Do you intend to update the anthology on a set schedule, or have you not thought about that yet?

A: *NALL* seeks to represent—though never exhaust, of course—a tradition. Ours is an effort at defining the boundaries of the Latino literary canon. Canons, as you know, generate love and hate from people, and they should. Still, any tradition that prides of being alive needs to explain itself to others. The Hebrew Bible is a compendium of books that were incorporated to the canon throughout time. Some were left out: the Apocrypha, which include 1 and 2 Esdras, Tobit, Judith, Ecclesiasticus, and Baruch. That is, every anthology creates its own double. Needless to say, *NALL* is but one canon-making tool in that search for parameters. As our tradition changes, so will *NALL*, by means of periodical updating in the form of revised editions.

Q: What do you hope readers get out of this anthology?

A: The span of possibilities that is Latino literature in the United States: ambitious, restless, forward-looking yet rooted in the past, politically engaged, with ties to Latin America, the Caribbean, and Spain, and, needless to say, in constant dialogue with other literary traditions in the United States. There is no literature without readers and *NALL* wants to reach readers of all kinds. This is a book about Latinos but not only for Latinos.

Sandra Cisneros

Sandra Cisneros

Los Angeles Review of Books (2012)

Sandra Cisneros is best known for her celebrated first novel, *The House on Mango Street* (1984), which is on school reading lists across the country. She has written six other books including *Woman Hollering Creek and Other Stories* (1991), *Loose Woman: Poems* (1994), and the novel, *Caramelo* (2002). Widely anthologized and studied, Cisneros is, without question, a major figure in U.S. literature.

Q: Your new book, *Have You Seen Marie?* (Knopf), is ostensibly about two women who search a San Antonio neighborhood for a lost cat named Marie. In truth, the story concerns loss and how one woman is processing the death of her mother. In the *Afterword* to the book, you explain that the story grew from your own experience of losing your mother. Why did you transform this very personal journey into a book?

A: My stories are often based on a true framework, just the way a piñata is based on a wire skeleton, but I have to add layers and layers of details to shape and bring them to life. True stories rarely have the symmetry of a beginning, middle, and end. During the time I was mourning my mother's death, I tried to busy myself writing about other things, but nothing took flight. It wasn't until I gave up wishing I was anywhere but where I was, that the idea for this story came about, and even then it had to thunk me on the head before I could actually see it. I often get in the way of my intuition.

Ironically, I had to retreat from my closest neighbors before I could include them in the story. Like Giacometti, I could only see my subjects from a distance so though the idea came about from an actual search for a lost cat, a lot of the details were developed once I was alone at my desk, and later when I spoke the story aloud.

Much of my writing is based on the spoken word. Friends heard early versions of the *Marie* story as we swung from my porch swing, and then I took it on the road, and the story changed again.

I'm reminded of a favorite quote by Fellini, "The pearl is the oyster's autobiography." Each time I told the story of my mother's death I was an oyster adding another layer of nacre to the invading sand grain. Each telling shaped the story and allowed me to gradually transform a wound into a pearl. And survive.

Q: You collaborated with internationally acclaimed visual artist Ester Hernández to create what you call an adult picture book. To place the story in your own neighborhood, you both visited the community and Ester took photographs of the neighbors who became models for the characters in the book. How would you describe working with another artist in such a personal and cooperative manner?

A: Ester says working on this project was like working on a documentary. I have to agree. I knew what I wanted and could see it all in my head before we even took a photo, which must've been terrible for Ester; I'm a control freak. But she was a trooper. She asked me to point out what elements I wanted to include, and, of course, some things were left to chance, but my writing is all about the small details. She had hundreds and hundreds of photos by the time she returned to her studio. I had the idea all along that this story should shatter stereotypes about my neighborhood and city. I wanted it to reflect the neighborhood the way I know it, with its diverse plants, people, and animals so my instructions to Ester specifically were to illustrate the story in an unexpected way, to surprise the reader by working against the official story. I had a lot of fun working with Ester on the field trips. It was often hot, and we were exhausted and overworked, but it was exciting work. We drove or walked around the neighborhood, often asking neighbors if they'd pose for us, the story inspiring the models, and the folks we met by chance inspiring and shaping the story.

Q: In writing this book, did you develop a deeper or perhaps clearer understanding of the meaning of death and how we might approach the loss of loved ones in a more positive and creative manner?

A: Look, I'm not an expert on anything, not even me. That's why I write. All I know is this: contemplating my mother after her death in both fiction and essays, and creating an altar for my mother (currently up at the Hispanic Cultural Center in Albuquerque), was like doing a five-year sitting meditation. I came to understand my mother in a way I didn't understand her when she was alive. It allowed me to finally communicate with her, to make peace, and in turn, to understand and make peace with myself.

Gregg Barrios

Gregg Barrios
La Bloga (2009)

Rancho Pancho, a play by former *Los Angeles Times* journalist and San Antonio playwright Gregg Barrios, is about the short-lived but intense relationship between playwright Tennessee Williams and South Texan Pancho Rodriguez from 1946-1947. The other characters are Carson McCullers (with whom Williams and Pancho shared a summer home in Nantucket), and pioneer stage director Margo Jones (who was in P-town for Brando's Streetcar audition.)

Barrios based his play in part on previously unknown correspondence between Williams and Rodriguez. Williams used his relationship with the volatile Rodriguez as a model for the character of Stanley Kowalski and his relationship with both Blanche and Stella in *A Streetcar Named Desire*. Barrios chose the name of the play from the fact that Williams dubbed their home together "Rancho Pancho," wherever they happened to be living. As previously noted on *La Bloga*, *Rancho Pancho* was presented in collaboration with Classic Theatre of San Antonio and was directed by Diane Malone. The Hansen Publishing Group has now published *Rancho Pancho* in paperback.

Q: To be honest, until I read your play, I knew nothing of Tennessee Williams' relationship with Pancho Rodriguez. Are you surprised by this admission? Have others admitted this to you?

A: I am not surprised. In fact, that was my impetus to write this secret history. I, too, didn't believe the story when I first heard it. Even after meeting Pancho and his twin brother Juancho in New Orleans in 1972 while teaching at Loyola University, I couldn't get them to open up about the relationship, nor could I engage Tenn into discussing the relationship when I met him soon afterward so I figured the whole thing was fabricated or wildly exaggerated—a fiction.

Only after both Tenn and Pancho were dead, did I return to the idea when I read director Elia Kazan's autobiography. Kazan who directed both stage and screen version of *A Streetcar Named Desire* reports an altercation between Tenn and Pancho while *Streetcar* was in rehearsal. Kazan used the incident to understand the dynamic of the play that was eluding him: "If Tenn was Blanche, then Pancho was Stanley," and he was then able to direct the play in earnest. That, too, became my mantra as I began my research armed with the knowledge that their relationship had been real.

Of course once I began knocking on people's doors to learn more, I was told by Williams' scholars and biographers—and friends—that I was confusing Pancho with Frank Merlo, Williams long-time partner after Rodriguez.

Even more amazing was discovering that Pancho was from Eagle Pass, Texas, just a hop and a skip from Crystal City, Texas, flagship capital of La Raza Unida, where I had taught drama and journalism for eight years. Ultimately, my good friend the actor Peter González—who is from the area, and starred as the young Fellini in *Roma*—related that Pancho was his uncle. He made contact with the Rodriguez family possible. Small world, verdad?

Q: The play is quite funny at times. Did you intend this or did this element naturally flow from the characters involved?

A: In many of the Q&A's that we have after a performance, I start out by asking the audience, "Did you find it funny?"

Humor is the dramatist's saving grace. It's an important ingredient. There has to be a balance. Heaven forbid, that life would be grim and unrelenting. Oscar Wilde used humor in the face of outrageous fortune, and Tenn and Pancho used humor, call it camp if you like, but it is in the humor that you can see the love and the bond, and then understand why the loss of love and separation become so tragic.

That harkens to the still modern Cervantes who used comedy in *Don Quijote* to tell the sad tale of his "mad" caballero.

Q: One of my favorite scenes in the play is when Marlon Brando makes a cameo. Was it difficult to write lines for such an iconic actor?

A: Well, as Tennessee says in the play, "You have to write what you know." As Pancho says about the Stanley character, "I just think there might be a little bit of me in him." Actually, I have Brando off-stage during his cameo for the simple reason that having an actor portray him might have dashed the audience's expectations. We all have our own idea of what Brando was like so don't spoil the magic. Actually, the real Brando did repair the electricity and plumbing at Rancho Pancho on that fated day. Hilarious.

We had the actor Bennie Briseño, who portrayed Pancho make a recording of his interpretation of Brando doing Stanley—sort of a mirror looking into the mirror, etc. It was quite effective especially when Pancho eavesdrops while Brando's audition is taking place off-stage. It is also very moving.

Q: Pancho is, in many ways, a tragic figure, someone who could have become quite famous if he were alive today. Do you agree, or am I just reading something into the play that isn't there?

A: That's hard to answer. In the context of the play, he is a tragic figure. I don't think he would have been famous if he were alive today. He kept his relationship with Williams under wraps. He wasn't one to kiss and tell, and you have to add to that mix, the entire stigma attached to gay Latinos by the culture. When I finally got Juancho, his brother, to open up about the affair, he, too, was reluctant.

Pancho was booted out of the military during WWII after serving two years in the South Pacific because he dared confide with an officer about his sexuality.

It is "Don't Ask, Don't Tell" happening 40 years before our present military policy. As a result, he received no GI benefits, and he couldn't face his family. That's why I included the scene where Pancho while tooling around in Irene Mayer Selznick's convertible gives a ride to a hitch-hiking Audie Murphy, the most decorated soldier of WWII, and laments not his own fate, but the way Murphy was treated in Hollywood, the irony is devastating.

Another aspect of Pancho's openness is the debate over gay marriage. He tells Tenn in the play—as he did in real life and in his letters—that Williams is the one he wants to share his life with "para siempre." If that isn't a heart-breaking marriage proposal then what is?

What many people don't know but as the play gets produced in other venues and other media (I wish I could talk about this, but my lips are sealed), they might come to know the true history of Pancho Rodriguez.

I have a proposal for a short Penguin Lives style biography of Pancho under consideration. In my research, I acquired a sizable trove of letters, photos, and personal mementos from his life. I truly believe we have to write our own stories many of which have been usurped and appropriated by others.

As Sal Castro tells his students in the film *Walkout*: "We were at Gettysburg during the Civil War, but you won't find us in the history book. Why?" Ditto the recent flap about the absence of Latinos in Ken Burns' *The War*. I would add, we were at the creation of one of the greatest plays of the 20th century, but you'd never know it.

Pancho figures in the forthcoming second volume of the definitive biography *The Unknown Tennessee Williams* by the late Lyle Leverich. The book's publisher signed *New Yorker* drama critic John Lahr to write the second volume, tentatively titled *Tennessee*. In conversation with Lahr, he has expressed great interest in restoring the profound influence Pancho had on Williams.

For my part, I have started a *Tenn Trilogy: Three plays about Williams*. *Rancho Pancho* is the first. *Tennessee Mon Amour* the second, and *The City that Time Forgot* the third.

I have finished the first and the third and am halfway through the second. The last play takes place 30 years after the breakup chronicled in *Rancho Pancho*. It opens as Tenn and Pancho meet in New Orleans on Jackson Square—just a block from the house where they lived and where Williams wrote *Streetcar*. It's all based on a true encounter. It's both hilarious and heart-breaking.

Q: Was it difficult getting *Rancho Pancho* produced for the stage? Were you surprised by the critical acclaim it received? Did you edit the play after watching the play performed?

A: It wasn't as difficult getting it produced, as it was time-consuming. The writing was the easiest part. Researching and getting the voices right took the most time. I got a Gateways-Ford Foundation grant through the Guadalupe Cultural Arts Center in San Antonio to develop the play—a commission of sorts. The play went through several readings, and each time I found ways to make it leaner. I originally had Juancho, Pancho's twin brother, as a character and narrator. After we presented the play as a staged reading in San Antonio and New Orleans, we got excellent feedback. I was privileged to work with director Diane Malone, who gave the best advice during this editing process. In many ways she was also the play's dramaturge.

When I sent the script to the Provincetown Tennessee Williams Theatre Festival last year, they were pleased with my rewrites and accepted it as the only play in the festival not written by Williams. I approached several Los Angeles theaters to consider producing it at the P-town festival, but most felt they didn't have sufficient time or funding to mount a production and then travel to the festival. Luckily, Malone was involved in a new theater company, The Classic Theatre of San Antonio. They agreed to mount a full production and then move it to P-Town.

I was not surprised by the positive critical response to the play. I was, however, overwhelmed by the enthusiastic response from the diverse audience—young and old, gay and straight, people of color and blue-haired doyennes. The theater had wrap-around lines, and some had to sit on folding chairs, it was so packed. At the time, I wondered if the passionate response was due to the audience seeing themselves in the character of Pancho or if they were seeing a play that doesn't pull any punches in portraying the love and sex life of a homosexual relationship. After all, San Antonio is still considered a conservative little town by many—even in the arts community. In Provincetown, the thing that totally amazed me, and I still treasure is that the audience composed of mainly New York City and P-town fans of Williams was so enthusiastic that they applauded after each scene. Unheard of. Plus the *San Antonio Express-News* sent their theater critic Deborah Martin to review the play, and we got our rare notices the next morning via e-mail as our cast and crew went to have "coffee" with Eli Wallach and his wife, Anne Jackson.

Q: How did you go about getting the play published in book form?

A: Months before taking the play to the P-Town, I was introduced to Jon Hansen of Hansen Publishing, who had published works—mostly scholarly and historical—about Williams. We discussed a T-shirt and a poster, and then he suggested doing a souvenir publication of the script as a one-time thing. Well, once the play moved into a more central position at the festival and the notices from the San Antonio production were glowing, we were suddenly on the Festival poster front and center. Once the audiences at P-Town saw the play, we were on a roll. Later, Jon and I brainstormed, and he decided to do a trade edition of the play. The more we talked, he decided to launch a new series: Hansen Drama. *Rancho Pancho* is the first of drama scripts that Hansen will publish.

Since then, we have discovered a very receptive audience eager to read new plays that perhaps they have no way of experiencing live. Once long ago, major publishers used to release reader's editions of plays. Hopefully, that tradition will now find a new audience.

You don't know what a thrill it was to go to Barnes and Noble at Lincoln Center in New York City and have a friend ask for *Rancho Pancho* by title and be told: "That's a new play by Gregg Barrios. You can find it on third floor, performing arts, under drama between Albee and Beckett," and there it was.

Better still, Hansen is publishing my new collection of poetry, *La Causa*, in October. I am blessed to have found a publisher who respects my work and hope that our literary relationship continues to flourish and prosper.

Aaron Michael Morales

Aaron Michael Morales

La Bloga (2008)

Aaron Michael Morales was born and raised in Tucson, Arizona, and is a graduate of Purdue University's M.F.A. program. He has taught creative writing, Latin American literature, contemporary literature, and rhetoric and composition at a number of colleges, including Columbia College of Chicago, Richard J. Daley College, Robert Morris College, and Purdue University. Currently, he is an Assistant Professor of English at Indiana State University where he teaches creative writing and contemporary literature.

His fiction has appeared in *Another Chicago Magazine*, *Passages North*, and *MAKE Magazine*, among other places. His first short collection of fiction, titled *From Here You Can Almost See the End of the Desert*, is the latest publication from Momotombo Press at the University of Notre Dame's Institute for Latino Studies. Morales is the author of one novel, *Drowning Tucson* (forthcoming from Coffee House Press), and is currently at work on his second novel, *Eat Your Children*.

Q: A strong thread of violence runs through the three stories in your chapbook, *From Here You Can Almost See the End of the Desert*, but the violence manifests itself in three different ways. Were you experimenting with violence as a theme?

A: Certainly violence plays an important role in my writing, but it's not violence for the sake of violence, or the ever-dreaded "glorification of violence" that gives violent art such a stigma in the eyes of people who don't dig deeper than their visceral reaction to people hurting one another. Instead, what I seek to address are cycles of violence, as well as what is at the root of violence and humanity's disturbing violent tendencies. Naturally, there are no easy answers to these questions, but I do think that understanding the motivation from each violent character or characters might help shed light on why some people turn to violence as a solution to problems beyond their control (or, worse, problems they can control). Of course, these stories actually deal more with the outcome of violence, or the lasting affect violence has on its victims and others directly affected by it. However, I attempt to allow the reader not only to experience violence alongside the victim(s), but also to begin to understand the psychology behind the characters inflicting violence. It's easy enough to say, "violence is bad," and leave it at that. It's not so easy to try to get into the mind of a violent person and understand why he or she opts for violence in place of a more rational response. Unfortunately, there is no shortage of humans who lash out at others irrationally.

All the characters in these stories who have been hurt in one way or another are so influenced by the violence that they begin to identify themselves in relation to it—whether consciously or unconsciously. This is what I hope people take away from the stories, how our actions affect others, and how we shouldn't internalize others' actions toward us so much that we identify ourselves by them. That is the greatest danger of being in an environment where violence is commonplace.

I also grew up in a violent neighborhood in Tucson, Arizona, where violence was just a fact of life. This leads to the other purpose of violence in my writing—a critique of the definitions of masculinity, especially the way in which violence and the ability to inflict violence are directly correlated with a man's "manliness." Where I lived—and of course there are tougher, poorer places—it was pretty much a rite of passage to be introduced to violence fairly early on. Guns weren't as prevalent as they are now, but there were no shortage of stabbings, beatings, and deaths. Of course, when guns did enter the picture quickly—and I remember it getting exponentially worse after the movie *Colors* came out in the mid-1980s, since all the gangsters needed to emulate the "real" gangs of L.A. to be legitimate—the violence escalated and there was a palpable fear in the city. It was honestly tangible, in every person's eyes, well, at least in the tougher neighborhoods. As I was saying, the whole thing in our neighborhood was that the toughest men were the manliest, and, therefore, reaped the rewards of being manly—respect, women, free reign to come and go and pick on whoever he pleased—and everyone knew these codes and adhered to them. As far as I know, this is very much still the standard. It's just that the sheer quantity of weapons and the easy access to them has now leveled the playing field a bit. Where once you had to actually be tough and able to beat the hell out of someone for respect, you now just have to be crazy (foolish) enough to pick up a gun and pull the trigger. This is what these stories address, in a roundabout way that allows the readers to approach the subject and dwell on violence, its causes, and their own participation in these cycles and codes.

Q: All of your protagonists are physically abused in one way or another: one by a husband, one by a father, and the last by bigoted teenage boys. Why did you choose abuse as center of these protagonists' lives?

A: Well, it just so happens that I have probably seen more abuse in my short lifetime than I can stomach, and it doesn't seem to be letting up. But, as I said earlier, I'm not interested in showcasing abuse, per se, as much as trying to dig deeper and try to figure out the reasons why people abuse one another. Also, to illustrate the fallout from abuse—whether it is emotional, physical, spiritual, or whatever, so if you observe the abused character in each story, you'll see that all three react to the abuse in a different way. One succumbs to it and internalizes it to the point that he doesn't realize he's now an abuser. One takes drastic measure to avoid further abuse and seek a sort of revenge for it, and one goes in search of an escape from potential abusers so it becomes important for us as readers to look at these three lives and wonder what would've been had they not been subjected to the various abuses they suffered.

Still, abuse and violence aside, I'm also interested in cycles in general—cycles of poverty, violence, drug abuse, racism, internal racism, sexual deviance, misogyny. All of these things intrigue me as a writer because from an objective perspective it would seem fairly simple to break, or break out of, any of these cycles. Yet sometimes those most negatively affected by these cycles are the very same people who perpetuate them. It's intriguing to me. But rather than just observe them—as with violence and abuse—I seek to understand them, from the perspective of those who are actually in a cycle and continuing it, and those who are affected by it.

Q: Are these stories the building blocks for a novel?

A: Yes. They are selections from a much larger novel titled *Drowning Tucson*. Francisco Aragón, the editor for Momotombo Press, read the entire novel and culled these selections as a sampling of my fiction to aid in getting my work out to a larger audience. It's safe to say that's happening already, and I'm grateful for his help, but back to the novel. It's roughly 400 pages, set in Tucson, Arizona, in the late 1980s, at a time where culturally some dramatic shifts were occurring in inner-city neighborhoods like the one where the novel is set. Some of it was the shift of gang activity from what would today be considered pretty mild and even petty, to the more hardcore stuff that has inundated almost every larger city in the U.S. Growing up in that environment at the time of the shift, well, as I said before, I think I can nail it down to around the time the movie *Colors* came out, which was also when hip-hop and that whole lifestyle first began to go mainstream. Acts like N.W.A., Ice T, DJ Quick, Too Short, and many others paved the way for the dissemination of "gangsta" life in places that already had their own traditions of street warfare, etc. Anyway, the book is what I'd like to call "urban literary fiction," as it is very serious writing, with very serious topics, but it doesn't attempt to sugar-coat or merely gloss over these lives during this time. It's a desperate book set in a desperate place and time., and I tamper with some of the traditions of narration, especially by employing a sort of hyper-realism to the scenes that are both physically and emotionally overwhelming.

As for the content, it's eleven separate chapters; each focuses on one character; all the lives are inextricably interwoven, though most of the characters are entirely unaware of this fact. Don't get me wrong. This isn't only a book about gangsters. In fact, the total page count they get is less than a quarter of the book, but that is the world this book is settled in. Still, the characters the novel focuses on are parents, lovers, lonely and lost people. They're impoverished, desperate people who want what everyone wants in the U.S.: an opportunity to pursue the American Dream. Other books that it could be compared to are Hubert Selby, Jr.'s *Last Exit to Brooklyn*, Irvine Welsh's *Trainspotting*, Carlos Fuentes's *The Crystal Frontier*, and Stewart O'Nan's *Everyday People*. There seems to be a great interest in this type of storytelling lately—with the success of movies like *Crash*, *City of God*, *Babel*, *21 Grams*, and others—so I think the novel's coming along at a nice time.

Q: Do you have a writing routine?

A: Because I'm a creative writing professor, I'll be honest; I don't have nearly as much time to write as I did in grad school or earlier. Still, I make a concerted effort to sit down a bare minimum of two hours a day. When breaks come, then I try to work at a more extended schedule. It varies. Right now I'm trying to tie up the loose ends on my second novel, *Eat Your Children*, and I hope to have it finished by this summer.

As for other routines, I'd say I'm in the habit of creating these characters, getting the basics of their lives down on the page, and then I stop writing and let the characters marinate—if I can say that. Yeah. They marinate in my mind for a while, and then when it comes time to tell their stories, not just illustrate them as people, well, that's when I return to the page, after I determine who they are and what they do in a given situation. It's kind of like dating or something. But they're not real. I also read when I can't write. Reading, to me, is writing. It's just as important as writing every day, if not more so. I always tell my students (especially the ones who complain because we have to read in a writing class), "how can you be a chef if you don't eat? If you don't try to taste everything, you'll never know what can be done." The same goes for writing, or snowboarding, or filmmaking.

Q: What authors have influenced your writing?

A: Too many to name. But I suspect readers familiar with some of my influences will enjoy my writing. I'd have to say the two most influential writers I've read have been Hubert Selby, Jr. and Gabriel García Márquez. But who hasn't been influenced by him? As for the brutally honest writing, the stuff almost too painful to read, it's probably most affected by writers like Irvine Welsh, Harry Crews, Bret Easton Ellis, Leslie Marmon Silko, Scott Heim, and writers like that. The more emotional and intellectual writers I enjoy are people like Junot Díaz, Jonathan Franzen, William Faulkner, Don DeLillo, Javier Marías, Carlos Fuentes, Luis Alberto Urrea, Ken Kesey, Günter Grass, and I have a particular affinity toward contemporary Russian writers.

Q: What are the more common mistakes made by beginning writers?

A: Not reading enough, and certainly misunderstanding the vastly important difference between revision and editing. Plus, it's hard when you first start to remove something or start over. It's like cutting off your arm or throwing your child out in the trash. That's almost how it feels. It's like, "I created that, so there can't be anything wrong with it. It's you who is wrong." Then, the more they read, and the more honest and unflinching they become with their own writing, the easier it becomes to revise.

Q: Are you the first writer in your family?

A: I don't know. I think so. But rumor has it that there was a writer on my mother's side, a great-uncle or great-great uncle, who wrote western novels. I feel like I'm telling my family's stories, though. While none of the stories I tell directly match any of my family members, certainly it's a large enough family that I can extract characteristics and apply them to fictional characters. I think a lot of writers do that. It's how we, say, understand how a middle-aged woman might respond to or see a situation, when we're twenty years removed and the opposite sex. It's what makes writing good. My daughter dabbles a little. Maybe she'll go on to do it for the rest of her life. You never know.

Raúl González

Ray González

La Bloga (2010)

Ray González is a full professor in the M.F.A. creative writing program at the University of Minnesota in Minneapolis. He is the author of eleven books poetry, two books of short fiction, three collections of essays, and a memoir. González is the editor of a dozen anthologies including, most recently, *Sudden Fiction Latino* (2010) published by W. W. Norton, which he co-edited with Robert Shapard and James Thomas. González kindly agreed to sit down with *La Bloga* and discuss his new poetry collection, *Faith Run* (2009), published by the University of Arizona Press.

Q: You have quite an extensive publishing career. Do you see *Faith Run* as being in any way different from your prior poetry collections? How have you evolved as a poet?

A: I don't think it is different from earlier volumes of my poetry, though there might be more poems about rock and roll music and famous poets that have influenced me. There are probably fewer poems about the desert Southwest and El Paso, Texas, where I grew up. I think my recent work has been more surreal than my older poetry because of the influence of prose poetry, which I write a great deal now, and the impact of the ever-changing poetic scene in the U.S.

Q: You divide this collection into three parts. What is the thematic purpose of this division?

A: In general, I find it hard to read a book of poetry, cover to cover, that is not divided into sections. In *Faith Run*, perhaps the opening section sets up the idea of a native leaving home for good and there are various poems about the art of poctry. The second section contains most of the poems written about older poets, something about their lives in relation to mine, and what I have learned from there. The third section has most of the poems about family and pondering the idea of someday moving back home with the sense that my faith in the desert landscape must keep up or keep running with me, if I do go home. The title *Faith Run* is about an older poet having faith in where he came from, while at the same time believing that the modern world of writing, publishing, teaching, and editing has things to offer that mean something to someone who grew up in a very isolated part of the country.

Q: One of my favorite poems in the collection is "Allen Ginsberg's Mother," which begins: "Naomi Ginsberg went insane / and never returned to her family." You go on to talk about Elizabeth Bishop's mother also going insane, and then you talk about your own mother who "whispered and prayed / for my sins." The poem is both funny and frightening and brings up interesting connections between mothers and their creative children. Can you talk about this poem a bit?

A: I have taught the poetry of Allen Ginsberg and Elizabeth Bishop a great deal and have learned that when a poet writes about family, and their frailty and weaknesses, that other poets are often good models about how to approach writing about such difficult topics. My mother was never as extreme as Ginsberg's or Bishop's, and she never went insane, but some people might say the deliberate censorship she played out against me represents the madness of the strict Catholic upbringing she grew up with. Such dogma does contain its own insanity, and to use it upon a young kid who was just starting to be aware of the real world, is its own story, though I guess it is universal.

Q: How did this collection evolve as a collection? Did your editor work with you in deciding which poems stayed and which ones didn't?

A: My books of poetry take years to put together from many individual poems, and *Faith Run* went through many versions because I am always adding and dropping poems. Though the editors never told me which poems should stay in or out, I had some good feedback from them on the order and sequences that made up the final content of the book. There must be at least twenty poems that I left out that could form the foundation for another book down the road. I have been fortunate to publish many books of poetry, non-fiction, fiction, and anthologies and people ask me how I can do it. Well, I published two books of poetry in late 2009, *Faith Run* from the University of Arizona Press, and *Cool Auditor: Poems* from BOA Editions, my main poetry publisher. It looks like I am prolific and lucky, but those two books represent almost five years of work and waiting several years for them to appear.

Q: Do you have a favorite poem in the collection? If so, can you tell us which poem it is why it is a favorite?

A: I like the opening poem, "The Poem of One Hundred Tongues," because it is about the lifelong commitment to poetry and how, as we write, we are sending out songs and sounds and oral words to a small audience. Poets in this country can't get away from the fact they will always have a small audience for their work. I don't mean only one hundred people but, the longer I write, the more I believe that we must remain loyal to our audience and work toward a sense of community without losing sight of who we are as poets. If American culture relegates small audiences to poetry, we must nourish that and acknowledge the poetic writing process is sacred and share it in a good, sincere manner.

Q: Another one of my favorite poems in the collection is "The Cardboard Box," which is about a boy playing with, well, a large cardboard box. This is something many of us did as children, but the way you write about it, the child's experience is anything but fun. The box "was stained, smelled like blood...." I also think that there is a great loneliness permeating the poem, and there is something sinister about that box itself. Could you discuss the genesis of this piece?

A: I wrote this poem because playing with simple things like a cardboard box often gave me more pleasure as a boy than real toys. Kids use their imaginations in this way, imagining the box to be other things, discovering solitude for the first time, perhaps. I think the poem is trying to show that simple things nourish the imagination at an early age and, the reality of blood and the suffocating world have the power to invade a child's imagination. That is one reason the boy goes back into the box.

Q: Do you have a writing routine? How does teaching affect your routine? Does teaching influence you as a poet?

A: I don't write every day, but I write in the mornings when I can because my busy job as director of the M.F.A. Program at the University of Minnesota and teaching wipe me out. I always write linear, stanza poems in notebooks by hand, then take them to the computer. This is a slow and deliberate process I can't get away from when it comes to free verse. I have been doing it that way for 35 years of writing poetry. On the other hand, I can sit at the computer and compose dozens of prose poems in one sitting, though I am lucky if three or four are any good. My old life in journalism and the fact I write a great deal of non-fiction and essays also influence the rapid process of writing silly, funny, surreal prose poems. It is a different way to work that has resulted in my third book of prose poems, *Cool Auditor*. My books of essays, like the prose poems, are composed on the computer from years of research notes and travels to the Southwest.

Q: If you were planning for a long trip where you could freely lounge about and read without any pressures, what books would you bring with you?

A: *The Collected Poems of James Wright*, Pablo Neruda's *Memoirs*, *The Selected Poems of Charles Simic*, *The Collected Poems of Elizabeth Bishop*, *Cesar Vallejo*, and probably a novel or two by *Paul Auster* and, of course, Bob Dylan's memoir.

Q: Are you working on a new book?

A: I am always working on prose poems and regular poetry and have been working for years on a book of writings about the importance of rock and roll music in my life—desert island discs, dead rock stars from the sixties, adventures at rock concerts, all of them presented in poems, stories, and essays. It is a multi-genre book and a hard one to write because music is so dominant in my life, and I would not be a poet if it wasn't for an important event in my early years. Sometimes, I find it hard to separate my response as a fan to the music from the distance I need to be able to write about famous cultural heroes like bombastic rock stars. In February of 1964, when I was twelve years old, I saw The Beatles for the first time on the Ed Sullivan show. It changed my life and gave me permission to rhyme words and silly lyrics I always carried in my head. I would love to edit an anthology of writers writing about the impact of music on their writing. Anthologies of poetry about rock and roll have been done already, but I would focus on more essays and stories about the impact of music on poet's lives.

Justin Torres

Justin Torres
Los Angeles Review of Books (2012)

I first learned of Justin Torres's short and elegant debut novel, *We the Animals* (2011), in a review right here in the *Los Angeles Review of Books* written by Rigoberto González. Rigoberto and I became friends a few years after he reviewed my first short-story collection ten years ago for the *El Paso Times*. Rigoberto has a tough eye when it comes to analyzing and discussing new books by Latino writers, and he will not give anyone a free pass. If a work is deeply flawed, he'll say so. If a piece of writing moves him, he'll let us know and explain why, so when Rigoberto trumpeted this young, daring author named Justin Torres, I took notice.

Then this spring, my literary path crossed Justin's when our novels were two of twelve books chosen as semifinalists in the 2012 Cabell First Novelist Award, which honors an outstanding debut novel published during a calendar year. When I saw *We the Animals* and other wonderful titles on the list, I knew two things. First, my little novel was not going to win. Second, Justin could be the first Latino to win this prestigious award. When the three finalists were announced a month later and Justin was on it, I knew he'd win...I had no doubt whatsoever.

It's been a year since *We the Animals* was published. It is now an award-winning novel that garnered raves from prestigious print and online publications. The paperback edition will soon be released. Justin Torres kindly agreed to an online interview while his life goes through yet another major change as he moves to Boston for a one-year fellowship at Harvard.

Q: It's now been a year since your debut novel was published by Houghton Mifflin Harcourt, and the paperback edition comes out this month. Since then, it has received the type of critical acclaim and press coverage all writers dream of, including raves from *The New York Times*, *The New Yorker*, *Esquire*, *Kirkus Reviews* (starred review), *Vanity Fair*, NPR, to name several. But I wanted to ask you about Rigoberto González's review of your novel in the *Los Angeles Review of Books*, which ends with this observation:

> It's sad indeed that *We the Animals*—like most literary works with homosexual content, aside from Greek mythology—will not make most high school reading lists without controversy, if at all. But even if it's kept off reading lists and library shelves, Torres's book will undoubtedly find an audience in a number of other communities, including the Latino, L.G.B.T., and both young adult and adult readerships.

What did you think when you first read that observation? Has he been proven right?

A: Rigoberto González is an excellent writer, and it was such a treat to find out he'd reviewed the book. I do remember reading the review, but don't remember this line. But then, I don't read reviews of my own work too closely. I can't. My eyes are near shut from wincing in anticipation of a vicious take-down.

I can say, anecdotally, that quite a few high-school teachers have found me on Facebook, or tracked down my e-mail, to let me know that they were indeed teaching the novel. But I've also heard from those who say they wish they could teach it, but the adult content is too heavy, or serious, or explicit, etc., or they teach certain chapters and not others. On the whole, I'd assume González is probably right. Adolescent sexuality is generally considered dangerous material for high schools to address in literature, which makes queer adolescent sexuality near toxic. He's also right about the book finding an audience through word of mouth in queer and Latino communities, and many undergraduate and graduate college writing classes, and these are all my people, and it makes me damn proud.

Q: *We the Animals* centers on family life of three brothers and their often bickering parents (Puerto Rican father, white mother) where money, food, and hope are in short supply. The youngest brother is struggling and attempting to hide his sexuality even as he sneaks off to public restrooms looking for partners. You've said that your novel is loosely autobiographical. How have your family members reacted to it? Have you been surprised by their responses?

A: Ha! What a question! Are you asking if my parents think I'm a toilet freak? I don't know. We've never talked about that part of the book. I do know that my family members have been variously hurt, amused, bemused, and delighted. I know they're proud of me, and I know they take issue with certain aspects of the book I've written. I have felt humbled and honored by their grace, by both the questions they ask and the questions they don't ask, and surprised by the support they've shown. I created a fictional family with major similarities to the family I grew up with, and yet this is a profoundly different, profoundly fictional family. I wanted to say something true about familial love and familial failings, and I felt the best way to reach that truth was fiction. I think, I hope, they get that.

Q: *We the Animals* just won the 2012 Cabell First Novelist Award, which honors an outstanding debut novel published during a calendar year. I am told that you are the first Latino writer to win this prestigious award, which will culminate with you being honored in November at a festival held at Virginia Commonwealth University, the sponsor of this award. Since you will be participating in various panel discussions and workshops during the festival, are you doing anything to prepare for it? Do you have any thoughts about being a "first"?

A: The list of finalists and semi-finalists for the V.C.U. Cabell Award included just magnificent writing. I never expected to win, and, man, it felt great when I did. I have done nothing to prepare, as of yet, but in general I'm pretty terrible at prepared remarks. I much prefer spontaneity and interacting with audience questions. Also, I'm more frank, and crass, and honest, if I'm not given time to prepare. As far as being a "first" goes, I always hope that whatever success the book has makes it easier for other writers, and other books, that may be marginalized from the literary center to find publishers and audiences.

Q: You've attended the Iowa Writers' Workshop, and you were a Wallace Stegner Fellow at Stanford University. How did participation in two prestigious writing programs shape *We the Animals*? How did your fellow students react to your writing?

A: Iowa and Stanford are very different programs, but they share utter devotion to the written word—the faculty, the students, the administrators, everyone cares deeply about literature, and the primary goal of both programs is nothing more than to support and nurture young writers. This is incredible. One could argue forever about the workshop model, and people love to talk about whether or not to get an M.F.A., and whether M.F.A.s are ruining literature, but I know that in my case I was 28 and desperately broke. They paid me to write. Enough said, and this is not to mention the mentorship, the fellowship, the drunken, sincere, conversations about similes and structure, the melding of tastes and the necessity to constantly articulate and defend my own literary tastes and choices.

Q: How long did it take you to write *We the Animals*? How did you place your manuscript? Did the process surprise you?

A: The book took five or six years to write. I say five or six because I never sat down and thought, I'm going to write a book. I started slowly. I actually finished right before arriving at Stanford, and was lucky enough to have published some stories by then, and through those stories my agent found me, so I handed the manuscript off; she sent it out to editors. I met with a bunch and clicked with Jenna Johnson, my editor. I dread talking about this side because it was easy for me. I had choices all along the way, and that is just not how it usually works. There are so many brilliant, successful authors who suffered through years of rejection. Rejection is the norm.

Q: Did you work closely with an editor at Houghton Mifflin Harcourt? How did that experience compare with the workshop setting?

A: Jenna is phenomenal, and we've become very close. She had key insights, but the book was short and tightly written. There was no major overhaul or anything like that. I was the same in workshop. By the time I handed something in, likely it was going to be as polished and near finished as I could manage. I've never been one to let people near my early drafts, not editors or classmates.

Q: I found heartbreaking your narrator's plight of being deeply in the closet to his family. When did you come out to your family? How did that experience influence or inspire you as a writer?

A: That's a long, rather tragic story. My "coming out" was different than the narrator's, but similar enough that to go into specifics would be too much of a spoiler, I think.

Q: You're now in a position to share knowledge with budding writers. What advice would you offer a young person who has the drive and passion to write fiction?

A: You know, I hate giving advice, and the young person you're describing, who "has the drive and passion to write fiction," needs no advice. Go for it. What I think you mean is, do I have any advice on how to get published? All I can say is that I had no expectations when I started writing. I wrote out of passion, or obsession. I wrote to break my own heart. I did not write to get published. I'd never heard of Iowa or the Stegner Fellowship. I didn't know such things as literary agents existed. I took a writing class, and I loved the teacher and the other writers, loved reading my words aloud. I read a lot, and I wrote more. I tried to break other hearts besides my own. I had fun with the work, and sometimes it felt like torture. I tried to be honest. I tried to write with beauty.

Q: You've had many jobs on your road to becoming a published writer, including working as a farm hand, a dog-walker, a creative-writing teacher, and a bookseller. Are you still doing odd jobs, or do you now have the luxury of being a full-time writer?

A: Right now I am a fellow at the Radcliffe Institute for Advanced Studies at Harvard. They give me an office and stipend, and the only expectation is that I spend the year writing. It is the oddest, most gloriously luxurious "job" I have ever had. After this year, I'll have to get a real job.

Q: Are you working on a new novel?

A: Yes. Slowly.

Q: All right, for my last question, I want to note that *Salon* named you one of the sexiest men of 2011, noting in part: "The intense, soulful gaze on his author photo, one that had literati across Brooklyn dreaming of meeting those empathetic eyes, earned Torres a second M.F.A.—as our Most Foxy Author of 2011." Will this honor be noted in the paperback edition of *We the Animals*?

A: I don't think it's on the paperback, but thank you for bringing this up! I try to work this into most conversations, but it can be awkward. Like someone will ask, "Do you want anything from the fridge?" and I'll respond, "I was voted fourth most sexiest man of 2011, after Thom Yorke." See what I mean? Awkward.

Octavio González

Octavio González

La Bloga (2010)

Octavio González recently published his first poetry collection, *The Book of Ours*, with Momotombo Press (Letras Latinas, Notre Dame University). His essays and poems appear or are forthcoming in *Puerto del Sol, OCHO, MiPoesias, The Richmond Review, Cultural Critique, Psychoanalytic Perspectives*, and other journals. González teaches literature and composition at Rutgers University, where he is a doctoral student in English.

Q: In his introduction to your book, Rigoberto González (no relation) recounts meeting you about five years ago at a "gathering of the queer literati at a Chelsea penthouse, where seasoned poets and novices converged to dialogue about craft and poetics as seen through the distinct lens of sexual orientation." Do you have any particular memories of that night that have stayed with you? Was this a turning point or milestone for you as a poet?

A: I do remember that night! It was an intimidating and invigorating experience to be in a room with so many talented and witty poets. I had been taking poetry workshops and working at the collection just released as *The Book of Ours*, which has been a labor of love for many years.

Q: When did you decide that you would become a poet? What kind of journey has it been?

A: I began writing fiction, actually, and only saw myself as a poet much later. This is all relative, of course, since my writing life started when I was in middle school, and I began writing poetry in high school. My first poem was awful! But, even though I never felt that poetry came "naturally" to me—I think it comes more naturally to some than it does to others—I worked on it, revising my poems obsessively. One poem in my collection, "American Sign Language," an unrhymed villanelle, has gone through more iterations than I can keep track of. Let's just say it began as two separate poems, and the refrains existed before then, as mantras in my mind, which wrote themselves, as it were.

Q: Could you talk a bit about editing your book with María Meléndez?

A: María Meléndez is an incredible poet and a warm, gentle, and visionary editor. She has helped me really chip away at the marble and let the forms and gestures and movements inherent in the poems come forth. We had conversations over the phone and went back and forth with ideas and suggestions. María was perfect in the way that she allowed me to edit the pieces while also guiding the wheel at important turns—I will always remember when she made a line-editing suggestion and then said, "Well, it depends on whether ultimately you want to end the manuscript on a hopeful note—it depends on your own vision of the whole." Her experience as a poet really helped me see the horizon or the "arc" of the collection.

Q: Who do you read? What authors have been your biggest influences?

A: I'm working on twentieth-century fiction right now, for my dissertation research, so I'm really interested in Junot Díaz, a fellow Dominican-American author. I'm also intrigued by the modernists at the beginning of the twentieth century—the lyrical modernists such as Woolf and the Joyce of the "Penelope" chapter of *Ulysses*. Two novels that really inspire me are *Story of an African Farm* (by Olive Schreiner), and *Cast the First Stone* (Chester Himes). I like my fiction poetic and my poetry prose-like—never prosaic!—and so I enjoy mixed genres and authors, like Woolf, who worked in various forms throughout their careers. In my life as a whole, poets such as Rhina Espaillat, and T. S. Eliot, Walt Whitman, Sylvia Plath, and other lyrical modernist and confessional poets have had the most influence on me.

Q: One of my favorite poems in your collection is "Fairy Tale in New York," which begins: "God squeezes but he doesn't strangle." Can you talk a bit about that poem and how it developed?

A: This is an old Dominican saying that my Mom always used as a refrain. I found it to be the inspiration for this piece, which, funny enough, is the most recent to go into the collection. I wrote it in 2008. I wrote it in one sitting, in a Starbucks in the Flatiron district of Manhattan, and I was fighting back tears as I was writing it at some points, mainly toward the end. My work is deeply personal, and I sometimes worry that it is too self-oriented. But that is the lyrical mode that attracted me to poetry to begin with. Ironically, this piece is the least "lyrical" in a strict sense, as it contains many voices.

Q: Do you have a favorite poem in the collection?

A: The title implies a book that is "ours," which speaks to the multiple selves (as the Anzaldua epigraph also suggests) that any one person contains. You can also hear the Whitmanesque echo in this theme—"I am large, I contain multitudes"—and the very Americanness of this lineage that I feel embraced by.

My favorite poem is the one (really two) called "My Sister's Book." Like the title to the collection as a whole, this series of poems alludes to the many voices one hears and is haunted by, the famous negative capability of the poet that Keats formulated. I feel like even those poems that are the most "me"—for example, the love poems in the middle section—are other "me"s, and I hope readers can enjoy this echolalia not as cacophony but as chords that touch the heart.

Q: You are a first-generation Dominican American. How do you think your culture affects your approach to poetry? Did you see a difference between you and your fellow students at Swarthmore and Pennsylvania State University?

A: My culture is part of who I am, and my personal history and sense of destiny and politics are deeply informed by my heritage and experiences, both as a child, and as a college student, and now as an adult. I see being an American as an incredible gift, perhaps because I do not take it for granted—to paraphrase a famous feminist, one is not born an American. Being an American, in the largest, hemispheric, Whitmanesque sense of the word, is a promise, a process of becoming that is never completed.

Q: You are currently a Ph.D. candidate at Rutgers, where you teach literature and composition. Has teaching affected your poetics?

A: I have had my students write a sonnet and now a semi-sestina—the former for a poetry-analysis course I assisted-taught, and the latter in an expository writing class! Part of my pedagogy is having students try their hand at creative forms, to invigorate their appreciation for writing as a mode of expression that is more personal than the college essay. I also deeply love poetry and poetic form and am a fan of sparking that love in others, if I can. I try to use my bully pulpit as an instructor to encourage the love of writing and reading poetry—cultivating the slow sense of wonder that poetry forces one to adopt.

Q: What are you working on now?

A: I am working on a series of prose vignettes that are autobiographical. You could say my current works in progress begin where the collection ends—the beginning of my journey when I set foot in the United States.

Reyna Grande

Reyna Grande

Los Angeles Review of Books (2012)

I first learned of Reyna Grande when she submitted a short story in response to my 2005 call for submissions for what would eventually be the anthology *Latinos in Lotusland* (2008). This was early in her writing career, a year before Atria Books (an imprint of Simon & Schuster) would publish Reyna's first novel, *Across a Hundred Mountains*, which was well received by the critics and went on to win the American Book Award, among other honors. Her second novel, *Dancing with Butterflies* (Washington Square Press), also garnered critical acclaim and awards.

Reyna was born into poverty in Mexico and was only two years old when her father left his family for the United States to find work. Her mother followed two years later, leaving Reyna and her siblings behind in Mexico with relatives. In 1985, Reyna was nine when she entered this country as an undocumented immigrant and settled in Los Angeles to live with her father, her parents having separated. Despite a life filled with deprivation and violence, Reyna has gone on to live the American dream.

Reyna became a naturalized citizen under President Ronald Reagan's amnesty program. She earned a degree in creative writing and film and video from the University of California, Santa Cruz. She then obtained an M.F.A. in creative writing from Antioch University. To this day, Reyna is the only person in her family to complete college. She lives in Los Angeles with her husband and children.

This summer, Atria Books published Reyna's memoir, *The Distance Between Us*, which offers a difficult read only because of the hardships she depicts in exquisite detail; it is a deeply personal coming-of-age story that extols the power of self-reliance and the love of books. Indeed, literature has made Reyna's life what it is.

Q: After writing two novels, why did you decide to write a memoir?

A: Even though my novels are very personal, and the material I write about is drawn from my own experience, they are fictional stories. After I completed my second novel, I wanted to write the real story about my life, before and after illegally immigrating to the U.S. from Mexico. I wanted to shed light on the complexities of immigration and how immigration affected my entire family in both positive and negative ways.

Q: When did you start your memoir? How did you map it out?

A: I started writing it in May 2007, while I was working on *Dancing with Butterflies*. I finished the first draft in April 2010, six months after *Dancing* was published. The first draft was very rough. I was cramming 30 years of my life into 300 pages! I showed this draft to a former teacher, who told me that I had four memoirs in there, and he suggested that I think about what I wanted the memoir to cover so I decided that it would be about my coming-of-age, and I got rid of the pages that had nothing to do with that. The hardest part, of course, was how to structure it. In the end, I decided to use my background as a novelist, and the result was a memoir that reads like a novel in stories. Each chapter is wrapped around a specific memory, a day in my life. I also decided to write it from a child's point of view with minimal intrusion from my adult self, just enough to guide the reader along. I wanted to take the reader back in time, and show, rather than tell, what my journey was like.

Q: You made a decision to include verbatim dialogue to tell your story. Obviously, you could not remember all of those conversations, particularly those occurring when you were very young. What convinced you to take this literary liberty? Did you or your editor discuss this decision?

A: In the very first draft of the memoir, I didn't have much dialogue. I didn't have a lot of description or details. There was so much exposition, and I was "telling" rather than "showing." My former M.F.A. teacher, who read the first draft of the memoir, told me that I had some latitude with my memory of the events and circumstances, that the point of the memoir was not to lay out everything point by point on a list. He said I needed to cut, shape, and turn this "material" into a story, so I sat down by myself and thought about what my teacher had said. Then something incredible happened. I heard my mother speak to me. She said, "I won't be gone for long." When I heard her speak, I had a breakthrough. I could so clearly see myself as a four-year-old girl watching my mother pack up her belongings for her trip to the U.S. Then the details started to come, so the key, to me, was to allow my characters to speak, and to give myself permission to recreate events from long ago. By the time my editor saw the memoir, it was already in its fourth or fifth draft. However, I was planning on having two separate memoirs. One about my life in Mexico, and one about my life in the U.S., similar to Esmeralda Santiago's wonderful memoirs, *When I Was Puerto Rican* and *Almost a Woman*. But my editor suggested that I put both stories into one book, and that's what I did. I was happy with the result.

Q: While you are rather hard on yourself as you recount what you consider your failings in the face of extreme poverty, bigotry, and an abusive home, you also don't spare family members, particularly your father and his violent alcoholism and your mother's abandonment of you and your siblings. How has your family reacted to your memoir? Did you allow them to read early drafts?

A: Neither of my parents has ever read any of my work. When I was writing the memoir, I told my mother I was writing it, but my mother doesn't really understand—nor will she ever admit—that her actions hurt me in a very profound way. My father was diagnosed with liver cancer while I was writing the memoir, and his illness definitely made me think twice about finishing the book. But, in the end, what helped me to finish the memoir was the knowledge that even though I was writing about my parents' darkest moments, I was doing my best to give them their humanity. Ultimately, my parents are human beings, very complex and complicated human beings with flaws and virtues. I am pleased that in the memoir my parents don't come across as the "villains" in the story. They come across as real people going through difficult times.

As for my siblings, I included them in the writing process. They got to read the different drafts of the memoir. They gave me a lot of input—filling in the gaps in my memory, correcting me when I misremembered. This memoir is as much theirs as it is mine.

Q: We've just survived another bruising presidential election where the Republican nominee moved hard right on the immigration issue, using such terms as "illegals" and "self-deportation" during the debate season for the nomination. Now that President Obama has won reelection with more than 70 percent of the Latino vote, many prominent Republicans are talking about softening their party's approach to immigration or else face future electoral defeats. What was your reaction to this year's debate on immigration reform, especially being a person who was an undocumented immigrant and who eventually benefited from President Reagan's amnesty program?

A: As an immigrant I've always been a strong supporter of immigrant rights and have been hoping for many years now for a comprehensive immigration reform. Unfortunately, that hasn't happened, but I do believe that now with Republicans realizing that they absolutely need to reevaluate their stance on immigration, the federal government can finally make some major improvements to our broken immigration system. In particular, I am very hopeful that the DREAM Act can finally pass. Obama's Deferred Action for Childhood Arrivals doesn't do much for the DREAMers. It was a good first step in the right direction, but these young people need something permanent on which they can build a future.

My family greatly benefited from the Amnesty of 1986. The day I got my green card in the mail was the day I was able to step out of the shadows. I went on to earn a B.A., an M.F.A., and eventually also went on to be published by one of the biggest publishers in the U.S.,

Simon & Schuster. None of that might have happened if I hadn't been given the chance to legalize my status. I am now paying back to this country everything it gave me. I believe that the DREAMers will do the same.

Q: You sing the praises of Diana Savas, one of your professors at Pasadena City College, who not only saw your promise as a writer, but who also encouraged you to attend U.C. Santa Cruz and gave you shelter from your father's violence. What has been her reaction to your success? Where do you think you'd be today without such a mentor and friend?

A: Oh, I will be talking about Diana until the day I die. I am extremely grateful for everything she has done for me and continues to do. I'm not sure where I would be today without having met Diana. I know that before I met her, I was very determined to go to college and make something of myself, but without her guidance, support, and friendship, I think the path to my goals would have been a very rocky, uncertain path. Diana is very proud of me, and, unlike my parents, she actually tells me so!

I love having her in my life because there are many things that I have not been able to share with my own parents, but I can share them with her. For example, when I met Sandra Cisneros in person—the woman whose work inspired me to be a writer!—it was an amazing experience. Yet if I had told my mother she would have said, "Sandra who?" But when I called Diana and told her about it, Diana understood what that had meant to me without me even having to explain it to her.

Q: Where do you see yourself in ten years?

A: Hopefully living somewhere else! I have lived in L.A. for 27 years, and I would like to live elsewhere at some point in my life. I would also like to have written at least two more books by then. I see myself being more active in my community and mentoring a new generation of writers.

Richard Blanco

Richard Blanco

La Bloga (2012)

Award-winning poet, Richard Blanco, is the author of four books: *Looking for The Gulf Motel* (2012); *Directions to The Beach of the Dead* (2005), winner of the 2006 PEN/American Center Beyond Margins Award; *Nowhere But Here* (2004); and *City of a Hundred Fires* (1998), winner of the 1997 Agnes Lynch Starrett National Poetry Prize.

Blanco's poetry has appeared in many literary journals as well as anthologies, including *The Norton Anthology of Latino Literature* (2011); *American Poetry: the Next Generation* (2000); and *Floating Borderlands* (1998). He earned his Bachelor of Science in civil engineering at Florida International University in 1991, where he also earned his M.F.A. in creative writing in 1997. While Blanco has taught creative writing and English composition at various universities, he is a registered professional engineer.

Q: Your new collection, *Looking for The Gulf Motel*, published by the University of Pittsburgh Press, is broken into three, untitled sections. How did you group your poems, and what themes did you hope to fulfill in each of the three sections?

A: The three sections are quite intentional, though I prefer to think of them as "movements." Within each one I was interested chronicling a particular facet of life from childhood into adulthood. I wanted to reach back and then look forward at how family and my culture have shaped and continue shaping who Richard Blanco is. The first movement dives into early questions of cultural identity and their evolution into this unrelenting sense of displacement that haunts me. How could it not, being born into the milieu of the Cuban diaspora? It's a perennial theme for me that started in the first book and continues to inform my work to this day.

The second movement, however, is something new for me; it begins with poems peering back into my family again, but this time examining the blurred lines of gender, the frailty of my father-son relationship, and the intersection of my cultural and sexual identities as a Cuban-American gay man living in rural Maine.

In the last movement, which I playfully call the "death section," the poems focus on my mother's life shaped by exile, my father's death, and the passing of a generation of relatives, all of which have provided lessons about my own impermanence in the world and the permanence of loss. Regardless of the focus of each movement, however, I see "family" as the glue that bonds the poems together into one collection.

Q: The poems concerning your mother and father are particularly moving and evocative, yet they are quite different from each other: you present your mother as a more active participant in your life (as in "Cooking with Mamá in Maine"), while your father comes across as more of a presence or image ("Papá at the Kitchen Table"). Was this poetic approach to your parents intentional?

A: Not only was it intentional, but it was necessary. My father, like many men, especially Latino men of that generation, was emotionally absent. He was a good provider, loyal and hardworking, but he couldn't express himself emotionally very well. As such, my father—it is sad to report—was very much a stranger to me. I have used my poetry as a forensic tool to study him after he died, examine his life, reconstruct him—all in an attempt to better understand who he was and connect with him through the page, at least.

My mother, on the other hand, was quite emotionally involved with me and the rest of the family. But aside from this, I portray her differently for yet another reason. In 1968, she left her entire family behind in Cuba—her parents, every brother and sister, every uncle and aunt—never knowing if she'd ever see them again. I connected to the longing and suffering of her exile that I witness all my life—and I wanted to record her "story," which is like so many stories of exile. You could say that I indirectly started writing because of her life and what it meant to me; as such, she is indeed much more "alive" in my poems, as she is in my life.

Q: Your poems concerning your identity as a gay man appear throughout the collection. But one of the most romantic (if I may use that term) is "Love as if Love," which recounts your love affair with a woman, which begins: "Before I kissed a man, I kissed Elizabeth." Thoughts?

A: I didn't come out until I was 25 years old. Before then I was romantically involved with women; I lived as a heterosexual male, and could have continued to do so. But I finally figured out that while I could love women, I didn't lust them, and I loved Elizabeth. Besides memorializing my love for her, I wanted this poem in the collection to show how blurred the lines of sexuality/gender can get. I think this kind of blurring is echoed in other poems about my family as well: my macho grandfather's tenderness, my mother's manly courage, my brother's fragility, and my grandmother's aggressiveness. As a Latino, I hate to be one-dimensionalized and, unfortunately, I think the same tends to happen when it comes to homosexuality. I wanted this poem to show the various dimensions of what it means to be gay—for me at least. Ironically, it was my love for a woman, Christy, that made me finally face my sexuality; I realized that I loved her so dearly that I couldn't lie to her; I couldn't live a lie with her.

Q: Cuban culture, music, and food appear throughout your writing. Do you consider yourself a Cuban writer, or simply a writer?

A: This is an easy one! I am an American poet who writes about his life experiences—the things that move and obsess him—like any other poet. In my case, these happen to be those questions of place, home, and cultural identity that arise from my "membership" in my Cuban exile community. I am a writer who happens to be Cuban, but I reserve the right to write about anything I want, not just my cultural identity. Aesthetically and politically, I don't exclusively align myself with any one particular group—Latino, Cuban, gay, or "white"—but I embrace them all. Good writing is good writing. I like what I like.

Q: You are a professional civil engineer. How does this training intersect, transform, and/or influence your poetry writing?

A: Oddly enough, engineering is largely responsible for me "getting into" poetry. When I began my career as a consultant engineer, I had to work on a lot of permitting jobs, which meant a lot of writing letters back and forth between agencies explaining often abstract concepts and arguing my clients' point of view—much like the sonnets which root back to legal pleas exchanged between lawyers. Anyway, this got me paying really close attention to language, how it can be crafted, its nuances, etc. In short, I fell in love with words. Also, the years of higher math and reasoning have instilled in me a strong proclivity for iron-clad logic. I find my poems are somewhat "engineered" in this way, sometimes too much so, I'll admit. Much like a musician who can "see" the mathematical structures in music, I see the logical patterns in language. I get a very similar kind of creative "kick" whether I am designing a bridge or constructing a poem. As regards subject matter, however, I rarely write about my "other" life as an engineer; it does not serve much as inspiration. I think that is because while the creative processes for the two overlap, each one has very different concerns.

Q: Who are some of your most important poetic influences? Who do you enjoy reading "just for fun"?

A: Elizabeth Bishop, Robert Hass, William Wordsworth, Neruda, Sylvia Plath, Sandra Cisneros, Philip Levine. Just for fun I read psycho-spiritual books that keep me sane: Alice Miller, Ken Wilber, Eckhart Tolle. But when the voices get to be too much, and I really need to check-out: *The Star, People Magazine,* or whatever else catches my eye in line at the supermarket.

Q: Do you have a writing routine? Where do you do most of your writing?

A: I am a vampire writer, often sitting down at my desk after 11 p.m. until three or four in the morning. Though I've heard many writers say they are "morning writers," getting up at 6 a.m. to polish off a poem, I think the idea is the same, namely, choosing a time to write when the day-to-day distractions are at a minimum. I write mostly on the computer at my desk in my home office. However, I scribble all over printed drafts practically anywhere, anytime—even while I'm driving! I find that chaotic, spontaneous editing mixed with the structure of focused, dedicated time at a computer is a good, balanced combination that works my brain in different but complementing ways.

Q: Are you working on a new collection?

A: No way! Every time I finish a book I give it all I got emotionally. I need some down time to let the well fill back up again. But also, I don't have a back pile of poems. A downside of having had my first manuscript published soon after it was written is that I have never had another "pile" of poems sitting around waiting to become the next book. Also, I've found that I am the kind of poet that has to let inspiration ferment. I often write about experiences several years after they happen. I need to let things "cook" in me first.

Daniel Olivas

DANIEL A. OLIVAS is the author of six books including the award-winning novel, *The Book of Want* (University of Arizona Press). He is the editor of the noted anthology, *Latinos in Lotusland* (Bilingual Press), which brings together sixty years of Los Angeles fiction by Latino/a writers. Widely anthologized, his fiction, poetry, and essays have appeared in diverse literary journals including *Exquisite Corpse*, *PANK*, *The MacGuffin*, *New Madrid*, *Fairy Tale Review*, *Bilingual Review*, and *La Bloga*. He has also written for *The New York Times*, *Los Angeles Times*, *Jewish Journal*, *El Paso Times*, *California Lawyer*, and the *Los Angeles Review of Books*. Olivas earned his degree in English literature from Stanford University, and law degree from UCLA. By day, he is an attorney in the Public Rights Division of the California Department of Justice in Los Angeles. He makes his home in the San Fernando Valley with his wife and son.